The Pioneer

Children of His Promise

Book 2

By

Ronna M. Bacon

Verses

Psalms 56:3. What time I am afraid, I will trust in thee.   4. In God I will praise his word, in God I have put my trust; I will not fear what flesh can do unto me. (KJV)

Table of Contents

Chapter 1

Clinging precariously to the rough rock wall he was descending, Logan Carmichael paused, his heart pounding, afraid to look up or down, knowing he would lose his balance if he did just that. He could feel the sweat tickling at his eyes and dripping off the side of his nose and refused to lift a hand to swipe at it. His heart pounded harder in his chest as he contemplated how far he had yet to go. The sounds of the birds and insects echoed loudly in his ears and he wondered at that, their songs sounded so distinct. He knew better than to climb down on his own but he just had to. There was someone down there and he couldn't see any movement from them. He could hear his older brother, Lincoln, calling for him before he heard pebbles trickling down beside him. He drew in a deep breath as his hand slipped before he caught tight to the small rock he had been holding on to.

"Logan? What are you doing down there?" Lincoln's voice reached to him but he refused to look up as Lincoln carefully looked over the edge of the cliff.

"There's someone down at the base of this cliff, Lincoln. I didn't see any other way down." Logan resumed his descent, inching slowing downwards, his hands and feet feeling for anything he could step on or grab hold of. He heard Lincoln muttering to himself and gave a grim smile. Holly was rubbing off on him, he thought.

"Logan? Did you have to climb down there?" Lincoln's frustration at his brother sounded in his voice.

"Well, yeah! How else was I to get there?" Logan paused for a moment to catch his breath and then resumed his careful descent, blocking out his raspy breathing.

He could hear his brother's wife, Holly, talking to Lincoln as he reached the final five feet and pushed himself away from the cliff, to drop to the ground and roll to a stop. He paused to draw a deep breath and then stood, absentmindedly brushing off his clothes as he stared around. He was sure there had been someone down here but where were they? He walked back towards the cliff, ignoring Lincoln's voice calling to him and then Holly's voice stating they would be down. She knew a path that would bring them out near him and just why hadn't he waited for her? He shook his head at that. Holly grew up in the area and had wandered the woods around her home all her life. She knew it better than he knew his hometown of Hope.

He searched, then stopped abruptly, a sharp cry torn from him. He moved forward rapidly, to drop to his knees beside the body, his hands reaching to touch the woman. For it was a woman, that he hadn't known when he stared his descent. He felt for a pulse, breathing a sigh of relief as the heartbeat pulsed under his fingers. He felt arms and legs and was relieved at no broken bones. He brushed back the shoulder length black curls and leaned forward to study her face. No, he thought, I don't know her but she looks familiar. Now, why would that be?

He didn't hear the quiet footsteps behind him until he felt the prick of a knife on his neck, stilling his motions. He waited, not sure who was behind him, but knowing it wasn't his brother.

"Pick her up!" The command came in a guttural voice from his left.

Logan shook his head. "I can't. We need the paramedics. If she's fallen from the cliff, then she could be badly injured." His body jerked forward at the blow he took to his back, the air driven from his lungs. "Did you really have to do that?"

"Don't get smart with us, boy."

Logan felt the knife once more at his neck. "Just what do you want?"

He heard quiet words behind him, too quiet for him to understand. Then he felt the shove at his back, sending him forward to land on his hands. He grimaced as the pain shot through them from the small nicks and abrasions he had accrued. He raised himself back to his knees, careful not to turn to see who had shoved him.

"Pick her up. She didn't fall from the cliff." He felt the shove again and then the man spoke again. "I said, pick her up. You are both coming with us."

Logan's head dropped for a moment as he contemplated his choices and then he shook it. Lord, I have no idea what going on or where we are heading, but You do. We are in Your hands. All I can do is what they say and trust You to free us. Just don't take too long. I don't think she'll last much longer, not by her looks.

Logan stood and then reached to scoop the woman into his arms. She lay limp again him. He studied her face, feeling that he knew her. She's about my age, I would say, but she's been through so much. He saw the blackness under her eyes, the thinness of her face. Her light weight told him she had not been well or had been denied food and water and that tore at his heart. He needed to get her out of there but he had no idea how that would happen.

He turned, searching for Lincoln and Holly, knowing they would stay hidden from sight. A slight movement to his left caught his eye and he briefly saw Lincoln appear and then disappear. Good. We are not alone. Let them have service down here, Lord, to call for help.

He watched the three men, or were they youths, who surrounded them closely but could not get a good description of them. The black hoodies they wore were pulled forward over their faces and he could see the dark sunglasses they had on. Just great, he thought. How do I describe them to the authorities? Then he mentally shook his head. That wasn't his priority right now. The lady in his arms was. He took another look at her face and frowned. She reminded him of Holly but how could that be? Holly had no sisters and he didn't remember her saying much about other family.

Then he knew who it was. Her cousin, Aveleen Dennis, had disappeared three or four months ago and they had never found her, despite searching for her. Holly and Lincoln had been involved in their own adventure at the time and he had not heard much. She wasn't from Cairn, Holly's hometown, so maybe that was why, he thought.

He walked as carefully as he could along the path that wove through the trees. He tried to keep an eye out for his brother but his attention was needed to keep himself on his feet and not drop Aveleen. Lord, where are we? You promised to protect us. Why do I feel so alone right now?

He was finally shoved towards a cave, through the entrance and then the men walked back out to hover around outside. He stared at them for a moment, before he turned slowly in a circle, not seeing another way out. He gently laid Aveleen on the floor near a wall, where she was hidden from the entrance. He then began a methodical inspection of the cave, praying for another way out and not finding it. He turned to contemplate the entrance, knowing that was the only way he could go and not able to with the men there. Lord, now what? How do I get us out of here?

He returned to Aveleen, feeling for her pulse, finding it weaker than it had been. He needed to get her out of there and soon or she wouldn't survive. He had no idea what she had been through. He sat down beside her, his eyes on her face before he reached to gather her close to him, cradling her on his knee, his arms wrapped around her trying to bring warmth back to her body. He heard a low moan and sighed. Lord, please? Anytime for help to arrive would be good.

He had no idea how much time had passed. His head was resting back against the wall, his eyes closed as he waited. He felt Aveleen stirring and looked down. Her eyes were open and he was struck at their colour of a dark jade. She was frowning, staring around before she looked up at him, her mouth moving as she tried to moisten her lips.

"Where am I?" He could barely hear her words.

"We're in a cave. I'm trying to think of a way to get you out of here." He frowned in turn as she shook her head. "I'll get you out and get you home."

"He won't let me go. He told me that. I have no idea what he wants from me. I don't know who he is."

"We'll figure it out."

She sighed softly, her eyes sliding closed, her face turning into his shoulder and she was still, so still he thought she was gone but the faint warmth of her breath on his neck reassured him that she was still alive.

He turned his face towards the entrance, seeing dusk coming. Lord? She'll not survive this night. How do I get her out?

Chapter 2

Logan stirred as he heard faint movements later that night. He roused, seeing dark had fallen, but there was enough moonlight that he could see faint shadows moving silently towards him. He froze, knowing he would not be able to put Aveleen down quick enough to defend them. He felt a hand on his shoulder and recognized Lincoln. He squinted, seeing Dougal Hunter, a police officer and good friend to Holly, with him.

"Logan? Are you okay?" Lincoln's voice was low.

"I am. But Aveleen's not. We need to get her out of here now." Logan struggled to rise, Lincoln reaching for Aveleen, Dougal's attention on the entrance. Once on his feet, he reached to take Aveleen back, shaking his head at Lincoln's questioning face. "She trusts me. She doesn't know you." He looked towards the entrance, then following as Dougal made his way out, turning in the opposite direction from what they had come.

He could feel Lincoln's hand on his back, ready to provide help if needed.

Once they were away from the cave, he looked back, a frown on his face. "How did you two get in there?" He kept his voice low.

Dougal gently tapped his chin with his fist and grinned and then pointed ahead. "Holly's waiting up ahead about a half mile. She has my truck."

Logan just nodded, saving his breath for the rapid walk, run almost, that they were in. Lincoln watched his brother closely, a frown on his face, not sure what was going on, but there was something. He knew of Holly's cousin, had heard her expressions of concern for Aveleen's disappearance.

Holly sprang from the truck as they neared, running for Lincoln and into his arms. He swept her close, his head near hers before he set her back, his hands on her shoulders, watching as she frowned at him. They could heard the night sounds of the forest, the twittering of the birds, the songs of the insects, the faint rustles of animals moving around.

"Lincoln? Logan's okay? But who does he have?" Holly spun to approach him, Lincoln's hand on her arm stopping her movements as he watched Logan and Dougal carefully place Aveleen into the truck and Logan jump up beside her before Dougal quietly shut the door.

"It's your cousin, Holly. Aveleen. We don't know anything yet. She's unconscious and Logan's not talking."

Holly spun back, her mouth open, before it snapped closed. "Aveleen? Leen? She's here? How?" She almost ran for the truck, scrambling in beside her cousin, her hand reaching for hers, a frown as she watched how carefully Logan cradled her against him. "Logan?"

"She's been like that almost the whole time since I found her. She was awake briefly. She needs medical attention, Holly, and fast."

Dougal spun his steering wheel and accelerated away from the area, his eyes on the area around him, not seeing anyone to cause him to be alerted. "We're heading that way. Holly, call Doc. We need to keep this as quiet as we can. If we take her to the hospital, they'll know that."

"On it." Holly spoke rapidly with Doc Aaron, the village doctor and a good friend of hers. When she pocketed her phone, she shared a look with Lincoln. "He doesn't want to take her there if he can help it. He said to bring her to his place."

Dougal shared a look over his shoulder with Logan before he nodded. "We can do that. Does he have what he needs?"

"He says he does. Logan? Did she say anything at all?"

Logan raised his head, his eyes on Lincoln, who had shifted in his seat to watch him. "Not really, Holly. It took me a minute to figure out who she looked like. The only thing she said when I told her I was trying to find a way out for us what that he wouldn't let her go. She didn't give a name, Dougal, and I couldn't get a good look at the men to be able to identify them."

"That's okay. They've been picked up by other officers. The chief sent them in, telling them to wait until we had you two out of there, or to move in if needed." Dougal pulled to a halt in Doc's driveway, watching for Doc to open the garage door and then pulled into it, the door sliding closed behind him. "We don't want them to know you're here."

Logan nodded, his eyes on Aveleen. "Let's get her into the house, Dougal. Lincoln?"

"Right here, Logan. Here, you slid out and then we'll get your lady."

Holly shot Lincoln a look at those words, knowing she would be asking him what he meant, then watched as Logan cradled her cousin to himself and walked carefully towards the door Doc was holding open. He laid her down on the bed in the spare room Doc had indicated and then stood for a moment, his eyes watchful, a frown on his face. He still wasn't sure they had been in time.

He turned as Doc touched his shoulder and nodded. "Let me know when I can come back in, Doc?"

"I'll do that, Logan. It may be a while. Martha left food in the kitchen for you. Ted's working on a school project in there. He may ask for your help."

Logan nodded, his eyes on Aveleen, before he turned, a prayer in his heart for the lady who had caught his attention. Right now, he didn't know if she'd live or die. That was in God's hands. All he could do was pray.

Holly was waiting outside the door and reached to hug him, holding tight. He felt the wet of her tears and know she had been weeping but she wouldn't thank him for saying anything. That much he knew.

"Thank you, Logan. Thank you for bringing her back."

He stood for a moment, his eyes on his brother who stood behind his wife. "You're welcome, Holly. I had no idea when I went down that cliff who it was."

"I know. You do know that was a very dangerous thing to do, don't you?"

He grinned at her for a moment. "It was? You could have warned me."

She gave him a playful swat before she turned, her arm linked with him. "Ted's heating some food for us."

"That sounds good." He paused for a moment. "Holly, how long was Aveleen missing?"

She shrugged. "I don't know. Two months, three? It could even be four. No one said anything when it happened. They were keeping it very quiet. I only found out when her cousin, Hannah, called from Riverville, asking if I had seen her. She had been gone about a month by then, wasn't it, Lincoln?"

"Something like that. Holly, you need to get off your feet. You also need to eat." Lincoln gently shoved his wife into a chair, his hand resting for a moment on her swelling abdomen.

"I know, Lincoln. I know I need to do that. I know I need to eat for the baby. It's just that Aveleen being here is such a shock." She turned to look towards the hallway. "Logan, what aren't you saying?"

"What?" Logan looked up at that, his hand holding his spoon freezing in place.

"Holly wants to know everything you know about her cousin." Lincoln smirked at his wife as he said that.

"That's right.   Although I wouldn't have phrased it like that." Holly shook her finger at her husband.

"I have no idea what you want to know.   She barely spoke." Logan stared down at the bowl of soup he had barely tasted and shoved it away, his appetite gone as he thought of how frail and fragile Aveleen was.   "Holly, did she ever say anything?"

"About what?"

"About anything.   What does she do for work?"

"Work?   She works in an investment company.   She does IT work for them, I think, or else she's a secretary.   I can't remember. It's been a while since we spoke, about six months. I'm not even sure she's still with that company. She was putting in her resignation and planning on moving. She didn't say why or where she was heading to."   Holly shared a look with Lincoln, who nodded. "Logan? Why are you asking?"

"Because it has to go back to someone she knew, something she saw, something she was asked to do." He ran his hands through his red gold hair, his amber eyes thoughtful. "She may not have had a chance to tell anyone." He saw the movement his brother made. "Lincoln?"

"I think you're right, but we need to talk to her. And if the chief shows up, we won't have an opportunity. Dougal left, but he said the chief was talking of putting her into protective custody somewhere."

"She won't." Holly's words had the two men staring at her as she chewed on her sandwich.

Ted Aaron finally spoke up. "Is she the one who spent summers here when you were teens?"

"She is, Ted. You know her. You spent a lot of time with us."

"Yeah, when you let me." He made a face at her. "But that doesn't explain why she's here when she's from a town four hours away."

"No, it doesn't, Ted." Logan stared down at his meal, his stomach roiling at the thought of eating anything more. He rose, heading for the hallway, seeing Doc standing in the bedroom doorway, staring back into the room. "Doc?"

"Logan?" Doc drew him away from the door and to a better light. "Were you hurt at all?"

"I took a couple of punches to the back, and one held a knife to my neck." He waved away Doc's assessment. "I'm fine, Doc. I've taken harder blows playing sports. How is she? That's my main concern."

"It is, is it?" Doc's keen eyes studied him and then he nodded. "All right. She's badly dehydrated. I would say she's not been eating and drinking at all or eating and drinking little over the last few weeks. Dougal said she's been gone for something like three or four months?"

"That's what Holly says. She doesn't know a lot."

"No, and it's better that she doesn't. Lincoln will do everything he can to keep information for her."

Logan snorted. "Like that will work. You know Holly better than that."

Doc laughed, knowing his young friend well. He turned Logan back to the door. "Martha's still in there, but go ahead. Aveleen has not roused at all."

"She was only awake for a very few minutes early, just enough to tell me whoever it was wouldn't let her go. She didn't say much more."

Doc nodded, a thoughtful look on his face. "She may not say anything at all, Logan, or may not for a while. It will take time for her to heal and part of that healing will be learning to trust again." He watched as Logan stood for a moment in the doorway before he entered the room, hesitation but also determination in his manner. Lord, I have no idea what's going on with these two, but You do. You placed her where Logan could see her, just how I have no idea. But thank You for bringing her back to us, to Holly, to her folks. Then he sighed. That's something else, isn't it, Lord? We have to call her folks and just how do we do that, given the condition she's in? We have a fight on our hands that I'm not even sure we'll win.

Logan walked quietly forward on his socked feet towards the bed, his eyes on the frail form laying there. Martha touched his arm on her way by, heading for Doc, where she too stood, heart raised in prayer for their young friends. Logan she didn't know that well but if his character was like his brother, Aveleen would not be alone in the fight she faced, and she had no lack of confidence that Logan had the same true character as his brother.

Chapter 3

Lowering himself to a sitting position beside the bed, Logan studied Aveleen, seeing once more, on her face, the devastation she had been through. He reached out a finger to move her hair away from her face, noting that at some point Martha had managed to wash it. He gave a small smile, knowing from his sister, Larkin, how women hated dirty hair. His hand reached to grasp hers lightly, stilling the restless movements of it. He waited and then leaned against the bed, his chin on his hand, as he watched.

He had no idea how long he sat there, Doc and Martha wandering in and out, not saying anything. He heard Holly and Lincoln in the living room before their voices too stilled. He thought they had left until he looked up and saw Lincoln standing on the other side of the bed, his eyes on Aveleen, a frown in place, before he looked over at his brother, nodding. Lincoln walked quietly away, his thoughts muddled. How did Logan do that? Doc has said

Logan had the same touch with Aveleen that Holly had with Lincoln, a single touch of her hand that stilled him and calmed him.

Logan's head finally rested against the bed as he slept. He stirred in the early morning hours, realizing that someone had covered him with a blanket at some point during the night. He yawned and his eyes searched the room, resting at last on Aveleen, seeing her eyes open.

"Aveleen?"

She jerked at his voice, fear, no terror, he thought, on her face before she turned, her features relaxing a bit. "Who are you?"

"I'm Logan. You're safe. We have you in Cairn at Doc's."

"Doc? Oh, no, you can't. I can't stay here." She shoved at the blankets covering her but she had no strength to move them.

He reached for her, scooping her into his arms, and heading for a chair nearby, the blanket that had covered him wrapped around her. He eyed the IV line and then nodded. It was fine. He sat, holding her as she struggled feebly to get away before she relaxed against him, her head tucked under his chin. He could feel the terror shaking her and wondered just what she had been through. He noted Doc standing in the doorway before Doc walked in and sat on the bed, his eyes on Aveleen.

Aveleen struggled to get away from him, to stand, but his arms kept her close to him. She finally subsided, leaning back on him, her breathing ragged from the exertion. He gave Doc a puzzled frown, but Doc's eyes were on Aveleen.

"I can't stay here." He could barely heard her voice. "He'll find me. They'll be hurt. Because of me."

"Who will find you?" Logan was truly puzzled, not sure what she was talking about.

"I don't know. I don't know his name. I didn't see him." She rested, her eyes staring ahead at nothing.

"Did he hurt you?" Logan's voice was quiet, even though his mind was racing.

It took her a few moments to respond, but she finally murmured a no. Her head grew heavy against his shoulder, but her eyes stayed open. Logan looked up at Doc, who shook his head.

"Aveleen, what happened to you?" Logan was frustrated, not being able to get a clear answer.

She gave a tiny shrug but didn't answer. She just stayed still, as if that was how she had had to stay for so long.

"Doc?" Logan's quiet voice finally broke through the silence.

"Logan, I don't know. This is out of my realm. I can treat her physical ailments, but there is something else going on. This is not her. She's feisty like Holly. Those two used to get into a lot of mischief when they were teens, not trouble though." He sighed. "I have a call in to her cousin, Hannah, in Riverville to see what she can tell me."

"Hannah? Riverville?" Logan was puzzled. "She's not from here?" He had forgotten what Holly had said

"No, she's not. She grew up in Riverville." Doc watched Logan closely, seeing how Logan was watching Aveleen and sighed once more to himself. Another one, Lord? What is it with these two boys?

You'll need to step in and protect his heart, Lord, but I suspect it's already given away. These two boys are like that. First sight and all, Lord. Just protect them both. Heal our Aveleen and help us to find who did this to her.

Aveleen finally slept again and she was tucked back into her bed before Doc drew Logan from the room and to the kitchen. He reached for the coffee pot but Logan shook his head.

"You need to eat and drink, Logan. I know you didn't eat much last night." Doc squinted at the clock and yawned. He should just be getting up at this time.

"Let me, Doc." Logan rose and made them toast, setting it on the table before he made himself a cup of tea.

"Logan?" Doc waited until Logan had eaten his fill and was sitting, cup cradled in his hands. "Did she say anything at all yesterday?"

Logan shook his head. "Not really." He shot a look towards the hallway, knowing he had to be on the road for his home that day. "I have to go home today and I don't want to."

"I know you do." Doc studied the younger man. "You're at the same spot Lincoln was, aren't you?"

"What do you mean?" Logan had an idea where Doc was headed with his questions.

"You know what I mean. You're restless, have been for months. I've seen that over the time I've come to know you. You're not happy with your life as it is." Doc watched with keen eyes the discomfort Logan felt.

Logan finally nodded, raising his eyes to the older man. "You're correct, Doc. I don't enjoy my work any more. I thought being a reporter was what I wanted to do, but it's not. And I have no idea what I want to do." He grew quiet, his thoughts muddled.

"Then, take time to pray. You may need to go away by yourself and do just that." Doc hesitated before he spoke again. "Someone needs to go to Riverville and talk to Hannah, to see what she can tell us. Maybe that person is you."

Logan's hand paused as he was raising his cup to his mouth. "It may be, Doc. I was thinking of heading that way. But just who is her cousin? I've heard the first name but nothing more."

Doc began to laugh. "She's the police chief's wife. You two share a name." He laughed even harder at the look on Logan's face. "You really do. His name is Caleb Logan. He should be able to help you in some way, if Hannah's not able to. From what Holly said, Hannah and Aveleen are close."

"Great.   Send me to talk to the authorities. They don't like reporters."

"Go in as a friend, not as a reporter. That's the best way."

Chapter 4

Turning the key in the lock, Logan tested his door and nodded. It was locked and he was leaving. He had given his notice at work and was at loose ends. Those loose ends included a visit back to Cairn to see Aveleen. Ten days had passed since he had scaled down the cliff and rescued her, ten days of Aveleen not talking. He had made the trip back there on three other occasions, sparking recognition in her eyes but not words. That bothered him. What had happened to her to keep her that quiet?

He quietly shut the hatch on his SUV, his eyes on his keys before they lifted to the apartment building he had lived in. His belongings were in storage for now. His parents supported him, as did Lincoln and Holly, but his sister, Larkin, had been very vocal at his decision. He snorted as he remembered their last heated words, Larkin not backing done from him at all. He shook his head as he headed for the driver's door, not seeing the vehicle that had pulled in beside him, the dark windows hiding the faces of the men watching him.

He pulled away, not looking back, not seeing the vehicle following him, his thoughts already in Cairn and on Aveleen. He sighed. She still wasn't speaking although Doc said her body was healing and she was gaining strength. He prayed as he drove, finally catching sight of the vehicle following him. He frowned and then searched for somewhere to pull off but finding nothing. He didn't see one until he reached Cairn and pulled off into a coffee shop parking lot. He watched the vehicle pass and then circle around to pull into the parking lot as well.

Now what, Lord? Where do I go? Prayer was a normal part of his life but he had never felt the desperate need to pray for himself that he did then. Why, he had no idea, but he just knew he needed protection. He left his vehicle, heading for the local grocery store, walking through it towards the back, nodding at the butcher who waved.

He exited the building, shooting a quick look around and set off at a rapid pace towards Doc's, ensuring he was not followed. Tapping at the kitchen door, he opened it and headed in, Martha turning from the counter to greet him.

"Logan? You're early. We didn't expect you yet." She reached to hug him.

"I finished up earlier than I thought. I'm at loose ends now, as they say." He searched her face. "Aveleen?"

"She's in the living room, Logan. She wanted up, quite demanded it in fact."

"She's that better?" He was surprised and turned to head that way, stopped as Martha's hand reached out to his arm.

"She's better, but not out of the woods yet, Logan. It will take a long time for that, Doc says. It's not just the physical healing she needs." Martha paused, biting at her lip for a moment. "She needs to talk about what happened and won't."

"No, given what she fears, she'll refuse to." Logan walked away at that point, intent on finding Aveleen.

He stopped for a moment to watch Aveleen as she sat, her feet curled up under her, a blanket covering her before her head turned in fright. He saw her features relax somewhat as she recognized him.

"Aveleen! You're up!" He walked slowly towards her, to sink to the end of the couch, his eyes not leaving her.

"Logan. Hi. I am, but Martha wants me to go back to bed soon." She frowned. "I don't know why I'm so tired."

"You've been through a lot and your body needs to heal." He prayed over his next words. "Can you tell me anything else?"

She shook her head and then sighed. "You're not going to leave it alone, are you?" She looked up as he shook his head. "What can I tell you? I don't know who it was. I never saw him, just the men who worked for him. There were two mainly, one during the day and one at night. They never let me leave the apartment I was in. I think it was in Cairn, but I don't know for sure. I didn't see where it was. I was unconscious when they took me in and the windows were blacked out on the rooms. I heard them talking one day." She paused, her brow furrowed as she thought. "They wanted something from me, something I knew, but I don't know what it is. I was a secretary and didn't do any of the investments or even deal with them in my work. I worked for a separate part of the company, the legal side."

Logan's hand paused as he rubbed it up and down her arm. "Was there something there that you knew about?"

She shrugged. "They wouldn't give me a lot of information when they asked, just kept repeating a company name. I don't remember it at all." She looked up at him, fear lurking in her eyes. "Are they done with me, Logan? Will they let me alone?"

"I don't really know, Aveleen. For now, you're safe here." He watched her closely, not seeing her relax at all. "Do I need to talk to your family for you? They need to know you're safe."

She shook her head. "I don't want them to know where I am. They'll want to come to me."

"Did they threaten your family?" He waited until she finally looked up and nodded. "Okay. Now that I know that I can take precautions for them."

"Logan? What do you mean?"

"It means I go there and talk to them." He reached for her hand, holding it tight for a moment. "I promise. I will not tell them where you are. Holly has given me some of the information I need."

"Logan, you can't. You can't tell them I'm okay." She began to shake with fear.

"I have to, Aveleen.   I promise I wouldn't tell them where you are."

She finally struggled to turn her hand over and clutched at his. "Take me with you? Please?"

He shook his head. "This first time, you're not up to it if we run into any trouble. I'll go, stay a few days and then come find you again to take you back.   Does that work?"

She studied him for a moment. "You promise? You'll come back for me? You won't forget me?" Her words were barely audible.

"I'll never forget you.   That's a promise." His voice was equally low as he watched her face, seeing a frown first and then the glimmer of a smile. "Now, I can get your family information from Holly or I can get it from you."

She stared at him for a moment. "Holly? You know Holly?"

Logan began to laugh. "I do. She's married to my brother, Lincoln." He paused, his head tilting as he watched her take that in. "You didn't know that?"

She shook her head. "They've been here. I didn't know that was your brother." She studied him. "Now that I know that, I can see the resemblance between you two." She sighed. "Logan, did they catch the men?"

"They found some of them but those men are not talking. We don't know who is behind it or why." He studied their hands for a moment. "We do need to talk about that, but you're not ready yet. I don't know when you will be. All I want is to solve this and get you safe and home to your family."

She nodded. "Talk to my cousin, Hannah and her husband. They'll help." Her head went back as she groaned. "That won't work. If you talk to him, then all the others will want to become involved and

Abe's men will want to come here and rescue me."

"It's that bad?"

She nodded, her eyes big as she looked over at him. "Do you know what it's like having at least 17 big brothers?"

"Seventeen?" He started to laugh. "No way."

She nodded again. "There's Caleb, his brother, two other officers, a paramedic and then four others plus a security team of eight. I don't have to worry about any dates making trouble for me. And that doesn't include my Dad and two brothers. Or the fathers of two of the men."

"And that's why you don't date?" He laughed harder. "I wouldn't want to run that gauntlet."

"But you see, going there, that's exactly what you will do." She sighed, her head dropping forward. "I can't let you do that."

"I didn't ask you to let me do it. I volunteered." He pulled out his phone and brought up his note taking application.

"Here. Write down all the names of the people I need to talk to."

She shook her head. "I can't let you."

"You can. I'm heading there anyway. I quit my job this morning and I'm looking for a new town. Riverville might just be it."

"You quit your job? Just what did you do?"

"I was a reporter."

"A reporter? Just great. Just what I need."

"Why? I'm not writing about you, if that's what you're worried about."

She shook her head. "No, it's not that. There's something I can't remember and it involved a reporter. Does that make any sense?"

"It does. Lincoln and Holly went through something like this."

"I know. I don't want to do the same." Her tone was disgruntled and she wore a frown.

Logan began to laugh again, bringing Martha to the door, asking what was so funny.

"Aveleen doesn't want to go through what her cousin did. I think it's too late to be saying that."

Martha gave a laugh, then came over and sat on the arm of the couch, her arm around Aveleen's shoulders. "I know you don't, dear, but I don't think you can avoid it now, you know."

"I know I can't. I just wish God had chosen otherwise. I don't like this. This is putting so many people at risk." She bit at her lip, frowning. "Now, how did I know that?"

Logan had leaned forward. "Are you remembering anything at all?"

She stared at him as she thought through his words. "Just bits and pieces. More than I had but not enough to bring in a clear picture."

He nodded. "That's that, then. Okay. I'll be gone for a couple of days. Martha knows how to get in touch with me if you need to." He rose, his eyes on her before he turned and walked away.

Martha watched Aveleen closely, seeing the look that had come over her face, a look that said she would be lost without him.

Chapter 5

His head turning from side to side to watch for traffic and also inspect the older buildings, Logan felt content for the first time in years as he slowly matched the speed of the vehicles moving down the main street of Riverville. He sighed. What was really going on with him, he wondered?

He found a place to park and shut his door behind him, a hand on the car roof for a moment before he walked towards a local business, stopping to look into the window before he moved on to the next window and then the next. He stopped for a moment, feeling eyes on him and searched but could see no one. Finally heading towards a café he had spotted on the way into town, he paused for a moment, a frown in place. Now that he was here, he was unsure about how to approach Aveleen's family. Maybe she was right and he shouldn't. He shook his head as he pulled the cafe door open and entered, his eyes searching the diners there before he headed for a booth at the back of the cafe. He slid into it, his fingers tapping at the tabletop before he reached for the menu. He perused it, smiling at the words he was using for his actions. Habits died hard, he thought. He paused, his eyes not focusing on the words for a moment, before he shook his head, looking up as the waitress stopped by him and waited for him to order his choice.

He sipped at his tea, his eyes watchful, narrowing as he watched three men enter and look around, waving at the older man at the counter before they headed his way, surprised that they stopped by his booth and then slid into it, forcing him to move over. He frowned, not quite sure what was going on.

"Holly called Hannah." The man sitting beside him spoke, a grin on his face. "She tattled on you to my wife."

"You're Caleb Logan?"

Caleb nodded. "And you are Logan Carmichael." His grin widened. "Now that's unusual to find someone with the same name as me, only in the wrong order."

"Be nice, Caleb." The speaker reached his hand across the table. "I'm Frankie Brennan. I serve under this guy."

The man sitting across from Logan shook his head, a grin in place as he watched his two friends. "You know, you're not giving him a very good impression." He extended his hand. "I'm Abe Finlay."

Logan watched the three men joke around for a moment before he spoke. "So, the police chief, a detective and a security guy. Where are the other fourteen?"

Abe choked on his food. When he could speak, he laughed. "Fourteen? What are you talking about?"

Logan bit back a grin, not wanting to play his hand. "Aveleen told me she has two brothers, a father, and seventeen other brothers."

"Seventeen?" Caleb shared a look with his friends. "What is she talking about?"

Logan finally gave in and stared laughing, startling the others. "Let's see. How did she put it? The police chief, two detectives, a paramedic, four others, and eight security men. Oh yeah. Caleb's brother as well. Plus the fathers of two of the men. To say nothing of her own father and brothers."

The three men stared at each other before turning their attention to Logan, a puzzled look on their faces.

"When did she say that?" Caleb was shaking his head. "There is no way she'd say that. Not our Aveleen."

"My Aveleen would." Logan bit into his burger, not catching the look the men shared again. When he swallowed his bite, he looked up, seeing them staring at him. "What?"

"Your Aveleen?" Frankie questioned him.

"My Aveleen. She's not the same person she was five months ago. Whatever she went through has changed her. Holly has even mentioned that as have Doc, Martha and Ted. Dougal is digging around, trying to get her to talk and she won't. I'm the only one she has said anything to." Logan looked down at his plate, unable to eat anything more. "Excuse me, Caleb. I need to leave."

Caleb watched as Logan walked away, stopping at the counter before he left, not quite sure what had just happened.

"Caleb?" Abe's voice brought his attention to his friend.

"Abe, I really don't know. I don't think she'd change that much, but you just don't know." He was on his feet and out of the cafe, looking for Logan.

Logan had stopped in front of the local newspaper office, his face thoughtful as he studied the display, before he spoke to Caleb who had approached him.

"She's changed, Caleb. She's not the person she was five months ago. She's terrified of someone and doesn't know who. She was starved. I didn't think she would make it."

"She was that bad? Holly never told Hannah, just that she had been found and was safe."

"I suspect Holly didn't want to worry Hannah. It was that bad. I scaled down a cliff to find her and was taken captive myself. Doc worked hard to save her. She had given up, I think, and it was only God that got her through to now." He slanted a glance at Caleb. "She wanted to come with me. I had to talk her out of it."

"Now that I can't see happening. She never lets anyone talk her out of something she is determined to do." Caleb paused, raising a prayer for his cousin, as Logan shook his head. "Is it that bad?"

Logan shrugged. "I didn't know her before so I have no idea how changed she is. Holly says she is."

Caleb studied Logan for a moment, realizing he was speaking the truth as it was. "I never thought she would change. It's a surprise. But given what she could have gone through…". His voice died away as he heard raised voices and he spun to see what the altercation was.

Logan turned abruptly as well, hearing the voices, and was off across the road in long rapid strides, dodging traffic with a hand held up. Caleb heard Logan say, "Aveleen", and then shook his head and was off after him.

Logan searched the people coming towards him, still hearing Aveleen's voice. He finally saw Ted and frowned, not understanding why Ted would be there, let alone Aveleen.

Aveleen searched for Logan, panic and terror beginning to set in. She didn't speak to the passersby who called her by name and welcomed her home. She had one objective in her mind and that was to find Logan. She needed to be with him and she had no idea why. She knew Ted was behind her, could hear his voice asking her to slow down and he would help her search.

She kept calling for Logan in a soft voice, Ted assuring her they would find him but they should have waited for him to return, just like he said he would.

"He's not coming back, Ted. He's gone, just like everyone else. Oh, what am I to do? I thought it would be easy to find him."

"He was coming back, Aveleen. He promised. Logan doesn't break a promise."

"He doesn't? Then, where is he? He didn't come back."

"Aveleen, he only left a few hours ago. Did you really think he could be here and back in that length of time?"

She stopped, spinning back to stare at him. "It's only a little while? I thought he

was gone for days. Ted, I need to find him.
And I don't know why."

Ted touched her shoulder, seeing the
fear deep in her eyes. "We'll find him,
Aveleen. But you can't keep running like
this. You're not that strong."

She shook her head, spun and began to
almost run along the sidewalk, her eyes
searching for Logan, the only one she felt
who could calm her.

She jerked as a hand gently stopped
her forward motion and a voice she
recognized but could not put a name to
spoke to her.

Dave Allison, a local paramedic, had
been heading for his wife's bakeshop when
he saw Aveleen heading his way. He
paused, a frown on his face, not sure if it
was really her. His hand came out and he
called her by name, not expecting her fight
to be free or the panic and terror that showed
on her face.

"Aveleen? Whoa! It's Dave. Let me
get you into the shop." He ducked a flailing
hand, catching the grin on the younger
man's face. "Aveleen! Stop!" He bit back
a groan as she stepped on his foot and his

grip loosened enough for Aveleen to slip away and head towards the centre of town, Ted on her heels. Dave stared after her and then ran that way, seeing Caleb heading towards her as well. He frowned as he heard her cry of Logan and saw her run towards the man with Caleb, throwing herself into his arms, holding on as tight as she could.

Logan saw Aveleen and knew when she saw him, her feet picking up their speed. He stopped, arms open to welcome her, wrapping them around her as she clung to him, sobs wracking her body. A frown in place, he looked down at her and then at Ted, who shrugged, concern on his face.

"She was looking for you, Logan. She thought you had left her and had abandoned her. She didn't realize it was only a few hours since you left." Ted paused, almost in tears. "She had my car keys, Logan. I had to physically stop her from getting behind the wheel. The only way I could calm her was to bring her here, and I'm not sure that even worked."

"She was looking for me? I promised to come back to her." Logan's eyes dropped to the black curls, unable to see her face.

"I know you did. I tried to tell her that." Ted looked around at the other two men standing there, concern on their faces. "She thought you had left her and weren't coming back."

Logan nodded, then looked back at Caleb. "Caleb? Where can we go? I want her out of here. Someone's watching us." Logan had recognized the tingling in his neck, that he had ignored the first time he felt it and lived to regret, a scar on his chest to remind him.

Dave motioned. "Rylee's closing the shop shortly. In there."

Caleb's hand on his back shoving him towards the shop, Logan turned Aveleen and hurried her inside, Rylee standing mouth open before she looked at her husband, who shrugged, not quite sure what to say before he swung the sign to read closed and locked the door.

Logan looked around, finding a chair he could shove Aveleen into, before he knelt beside her, one arm around her, the other hand brushing at the tears on her cheeks, soft murmurs coming from his mouth.

Caleb watched closely before he approached Ted. "And you would be?"

Ted shot him a look, not quite sure what was going on. "I'm Ted Aaron. I had to bring her. She would have tried to come on her own. Dad called me when we were about halfway here. He's worried. He wants her to find someone here to treat her if she won't come back home."

Caleb nodded, a compassionate look on his face, a hand on Ted's shoulder. "She's determined. Always has been." He watched Ted's face closely. "What is it, Ted?"

"I think we were followed almost to town. There was a truck that kept just far enough back I couldn't get a plate number. It turned off about five miles back."

"Let me have the description and I'll put it out." Caleb grinned at Ted's confusion. "I'm the police chief. Caleb Logan."

"Caleb Logan? Aveleen's cousin's husband? I didn't know you were the chief here."

"I am. Here, Rylee has something for you to eat. Sit. I need to talk to Aveleen, if she'll let me." He grinned again as Ted shook his head. "You don't think she will?"

"No, I don't. The only one she has talked to or will talk to is Logan. She was so stressed and panicked this morning after he left. I couldn't stop her from coming. I tried."

"We know you did, Ted. You did the right thing by bringing her, not letting her come on her own. That was not an easy decision, now was it?" Caleb watched closely, seeing the relief slide across Ted's face.

"You understand?" At Caleb's nod, he sighed. "I was so afraid I couldn't get her here without someone stopping us. And then I didn't know if I had done the right thing. Dad said I did, that I needed to be with her." Ted's words stopped, and he chewed at his lip as he watched Logan and Aveleen. "Dad's our doctor in town. He wants me to find someone who can check her over."

"Dave is a paramedic. He can do an initial assessment and then we have a friend who is a physician. He'll be glad to help."

Chapter 6

His eyes on Aveleen's face, Logan frowned, seeing how she was relaxing now that she was with him. Lord, what is going on here? Didn't she understand I was coming back? What happened to her over those months?

"Aveleen? What happened?"

She shook her head at his question. "I don't know, Logan. All I knew was that I felt you had walked away from me and I wouldn't see you again. I panicked, I guess." Her eyes sought for Ted, finding him sitting not too far away, absorbed in the snack that Rylee had provided for hm. "I need to apologize to Ted. He tried to tell me you were coming back. I didn't listen. I don't think I was nice to him."

Logan gave a small grin. "No, I don't think you were but you didn't mean to do that. You just had one object in mind, didn't you?"

Her eyes raised to his and she nodded. "You're the only one I feel safe with. And I needed to feel that." She heard a sound and looked around. "What? I'm at Rylee's?"

"That you are, Aveleen. Can you tell us why and what happened?" Caleb scooted a chair closer and sat, a frown on his face as he watched her shake her head. "Why won't you?"

She shook her head. "I don't know, Caleb. I don't know. And I wish I did." She stared at him. "There's a reason I can't and I don't know why."

"They threatened her family, Caleb. That much she knows." Logan watched Caleb's face closely, seeing it tighten. "Talk to Dougal Hunter in Cairn. He knows who they are."

"I'll do that. But what do we do with Aveleen now that she's here?"

Logan nodded. "I know. They're following her and they followed me. Why, I have no idea."

Ted had turned as he listened, his eyes first on Logan, then on Aveleen. "We were followed here, Logan. I didn't get a good look at whoever it was. Dad said he thought someone had been prowling around the house but Dougal didn't see any signs they had tried to get in."

Aveleen was watching him closely. "Your dad never said a word. Why not?"

Ted shrugged. "I guess he thought you had enough, trying to get better."

"Don't ever hide anything from me again. Do you all understand that?" She glared at them, not seeing the grins Caleb and Dave were trying hard to hide.

"They know that, Aveleen. Draw back the claws." Logan's hand squeezed on hers. "They're looking out for your safety."

"I know." She sounded disgruntled. "It's just that I seem to have lost some time and I don't like that. I also don't like the fact that I can't do what I want."

"We get that, Aveleen." Caleb shared a look with Logan before he continued. "We just want to get you well, get you safe, and let you have your life back."

"That I will never have back, Caleb. This has changed that. I can't go back to that person or to that life. Not ever. And Lord help me, I want to. I want this to have never happened." Tears sparkled in her eyes, surprising the two men from Riverville. They didn't remember ever seeing her cry before. She shifted slightly to watch Logan, finding his eyes on her. "Logan? Did you see the men? Did they say anything? Anything at all?"

He sighed, knowing what she was asking and that he couldn't help. Not that way. "They just told me to pick up you and that you hadn't fallen from the cliff. They made sure I didn't see their faces."

She leaned into his shoulder, feeling protected. "That's what I thought you had said. Now, how do I remember?"

"It will take time, Aveleen." Dave finally spoke. "We need to put you somewhere you can do just that."

"I'm not going to Abe's. Forgot that idea. But I can't go home and I can't go to Mom and Dad's." She struggled with that knowledge, knowing just being in town put them at risk. "Where can I go? Logan?" She turned, panic beginning to set in.

"I won't leave you. I promise you that." Logan's arm tightened around her. "Where can we go, Caleb?"

Caleb's face showed he was studying the question, trying to determine just where to put Aveleen. "For tonight, I would suggest Abe's." He held up a hand at her protest. "Just for the night, Aveleen. Until we can get plans made." He stood and paced. "Hannah wants to see you."

She began to shake her head in a violent manner. "No. I can't. I can't put either her or your children at risk." Her hand came to her mouth as memories flooded her mind. "Oh, no! I did it!"

"Did what?" Caleb came back and crouched in front of her. "What did you do?" Compassion filled his voice.

"I came here. They warned me not to." She looked up, fear and shock on her face, to such an extent that the ones surrounding her drew in sharp breaths.

"Did they threaten my family?" Caleb's voice was grim.

"I think they did. Towards the end. I just wish I could remember what they wanted. It was something to do with a company of some kind."

"Don't push it." Rylee finally spoke, bringing Aveleen's head back up as she watched her. "Relax. Heal. When you least expect it, the memory will return. If it doesn't, then we'll deal with it."

Aveleen sprang to her feet, wobbled for a moment and then paced towards the door, freezing in her walk as she saw a shadow outside. She gave a small scream and stumbled backwards, prevented from falling by Logan's arms around her. Caleb was at the door and outside before she could say anything. Logan looked around and then swept her behind the doors to the kitchen and to Rylee's office that she pointed to. Dave was on his heels, keys in hand.

"Out that door there, Logan. My car's outside. We'll take her to Abe's for the night."

"Why Abe's?"

"Because he has a security compound where she should be safe enough. He runs security team training and his team and their families live there." He grinned suddenly. "That's the eight men she mentioned."

Logan gave a brief grin, his eyes on Aveleen, seeing her starting to shut down, fatigue weighing down her eyes. He swept her out the door and into Dave's car, shutting the door quietly behind him.

Dave drove past the shop, a frown on his face as he recognized the man Caleb was speaking with, catching Caleb's eye briefly.

"That's Aveleen's father. Someone must have told him she was there."

"That's not good. Not with what she says." Logan chewed at his lip. "But we can't hide her from them. They deserve to see her."

"I know they do. We'll work something out." He glanced in the rearview mirror. "We have problems, Logan. We have a tail."

"And how do you shake it?"

"Like this." Dave suddenly shot off onto a side road and then sped back towards town and through side streets until he reached an office building. "In here. Emma should be working today and she'll get you two out to Abe's."

"And just who is Emma?"

"Abe's wife. They have quite a story." He pulled to a stop near the back door. "Out you get. Emma's seen us and is waiting."

Logan had Aveleen out and into the building, a smiling russet-haired woman locking the door behind them.

"You must be Logan. Abe said you were in town. I just didn't expect to see Aveleen." She studied the younger woman. "Oh, this isn't good. What happened?"

"She was spooked at Rylee's, is it? And Dave got us out of there. He said it was her Dad that spooked her."

"Her Dad?" Emma shook her head as she headed for her office and returned, her backpack on her shoulder. "Come on. Let's get you out to our place."

"Wait! I can't let you put yourself in danger."

"I'm not. Abe's waiting for us and he has some of the team with him." She stared at Logan as he began to laugh. "You find this funny?"

"I am guessing Abe didn't tell you what Aveleen said about all the guys in her

64

life?" Logan grinned at Aveleen, knowing how she would react to that.

"No, he didn't. Aveleen? Care to explain?"

"About the extra seventeen brothers? No." Aveleen was disgruntled and it showed in the tone of her voice.

Emma stared at her again for a moment and then began to laugh. "Oh! I can see what you mean. They do try to protect us, don't they?"

"Well, you have reason for them to do that. I never did."

"No, you never did, not until now. And they shouldn't have. But it's because they care about you and what happens to you." She stopped, turned to look at Logan and broke out into laughter. "He has no idea what's facing him, does he?"

"No. And he shouldn't have to."

"Hey, ladies. I know what I'm facing. I can take it." Logan just grinned at Emma's look.

Logan watched carefully as Abe drove them through the gates to his security compound, liking what he saw. His eyes rested on Aveleen, seeing her relaxing against him, the stress and fears dissipating.

"We're at Abe's?" Her voice was low.

"We are. We thought it best."

She shrugged. "I guess. Who was at the shop again?"

"Your Dad. He heard you were in town and there." Abe shared a look with Emma. "He wants to see you as does your Mom and brothers."

"Can I call them first? I just can't be near them."

"We'll bring them out here if we need to, Aveleen." Abe watched with compassion as she withdrew back into herself, her hand reaching for Logan. He was puzzled as he saw her relax at his touch and raised his eyes to Emma, who nodded, having already seen the effect Logan had on the younger woman.

She finally shrugged, then pushed at him to let her out, not seeing the men standing watching, first her, then Logan, and finally Abe, who shook his head at them. He knew his men were concerned, and that each one had taken time on their own and as a group to search for her.

Chapter 7

Aveleen rose the next morning, still exhausted. Enough already, she thought. I should be getting better and I'm not. I feel like I am standing still. She searched the cabin, not finding Logan, and feeling a moment of panic, before she refreshed her memory that he had promised not to leave her. Lord, I am so afraid. I don't know why or where I'm going on this journey into a strange, yet familiar, land. You know and You are in control. I know You have promised never to leave me but I am still so afraid. She jumped as she heard a noise and spun, seeing Logan closing the door behind him before he turned and found her watching him.

A smile lit up his face as he approached her. "You're up! Hungry?"

She finally nodded. "I think I am. I haven't been. What are you making?"

"Me? I thought women cooked, men ate." He grinned at her frown. "No? It doesn't work that way?"

She shook her head. "No. I don't think so." Her brow furrowed as she watched him. "Can you cook?"

He nodded, even as his grin widened. "Mom made sure we could. What do you feel like this morning?"

"Nothing, to tell you the truth." She sighed as she caught his head shaking. "You're not going to let me away with that, are you?" She felt lighter in spirit and safer when she was with Logan, and she didn't know why. She was too tired and down in her spirit to realize she was attracted to him. She had lost her ability to sense that.

He caught her hand, leading her to the kitchen and shoved her onto a stool at the breakfast bar. "Abe said he stocked the cabin yesterday afternoon, just in case. How about scrambled eggs and toast?"

She finally sighed. "I'm not hungry but I guess I have to eat, don't I?" She rose and hunted through the cupboards. "Don't they have any herbal tea?"

"That cupboard by the coffee pot. Emma remembered what you liked and brought some down last night after you were asleep." He didn't tell her that he and

Emma had had a long talk, Emma offering advice from her perspective as a friend and also as someone who had gone through trials.

"She did? Did she tell you about their adventure as they term it?"

"No, she didn't and I didn't ask. I don't pry into people's lives, even though I was a reporter."

"Was? You're not now?" She set her cup down and leaned her chin on her hands. "Why not?"

He shrugged as he set her plate of food in front of her and then slid his own onto the countertop beside her before he grabbed his mug of tea and sat, his hand reaching for hers as he asked a blessing on their food.

She didn't eat, just sat watching him. He pointed to her food and she still didn't pick up her fork. He sighed, reached for her fork, and then lifted a mouthful of food up, catching her with her mouth open to protest. She choked for a moment before she chewed and swallowed, her mouth opening to protest, which he promptly filled with another mouthful before handing her the fork and pointing at her plate.

She finally pushed her plate away and glared at him. He bit back a smile, knowing it would only worsen the situation before he reached for her hands, bowing his head, petitioning God for strength, for healing, for wisdom, for patience, and for an answer for what she had been through. Aveleen listened as he prayed, feeling hope for the first time in months. God, are You there? Do You really care? I felt like You had left me, had abandoned me.

Logan rose and headed for the door, hearing a soft tap. He opened it, stepping back to let Caleb enter, shaking his head at the question on the other's man's face

"She hasn't talked?" Caleb kept his voice low, his eyes on Aveleen as she sat, staring off into the distance, a blank look on her face.

"No. I just got some food into her and that was a struggle." Logan assessed the look on Caleb's face and knew what he was after. "You want her statement." His voice went flat, knowing just how difficult that would be.

"I need to, Logan. I can't let her go any longer without it. If I do, then if we ever catch whoever it is, her statement will be tossed out as compromised. None of us want that." Caleb paused, then moved towards Aveleen, causing her to start and then turn in fear towards him, her eyes searching for Logan.

Logan gave a sound and then was beside her, how he got there that fast he never knew afterwards. She reached for him and his arms came around her as he stood at her side, feeling her lean against him, and then calming as she felt his touch. Lord, I have no idea why this happens. But You do. Help us to help her. Help her to remember what she needs to so we can find the men responsible.

"Caleb?" The two men could hear the fear in her voice.

Caleb slid onto the stool Logan had used. "It's okay, Aveleen. I need to get a statement from you."

She was shaking her head, fear on her face. "I can't, Caleb. I can't."

Logan's arms tightened around her. "Aveleen, we need this. You need to talk to us."

She twisted so she could search his face, seeing the caring and compassion on his face, but something deeper in his eyes that caused her to frown. He nodded.

"You need to, Aveleen. It's part of the healing process." He raised his eyes to Caleb who motioned for him to continue. "If Caleb says it's okay for me to stay, I will."

She turned, her eyes on Caleb, who in turn nodded. "He can stay, Caleb? It won't hurt?"

"No, it won't hurt. I'll make sure of that. I just need to get your statement, Aveleen. It's been almost too long now." He reached down for his briefcase, pulling out a laptop and setting it up, and then reaching for a camera. "I'll videotape your statement as well. Logan can't be near you while you're giving it. You can't look at him, only at the camera."

"I can't? Oh, I don't think I can do this." She heard Logan's voice raised in prayer once more, feeling the calming effect of his words. She finally looked up at Caleb. "I will but I will only do this once." She pointed behind him. "Logan stands there, right behind you. I need to be able to see him."

Caleb shared a look with Logan before nodding. "All right. I will allow that. But keep your eyes on the camera, please. If you can't, then I'll have to ask him to leave." Caleb sighed, his eyes full of compassion. "Please, Aveleen. I only want to put you through this once. Work with me?"

She stared up at Logan, trying to read his thoughts, watching as his eyes softened as he nodded as well. "All right, Caleb. One time only is what I will give you. And heaven help you if I have to testify in court."

"That you'll have to do, Aveleen. Unless they plead guilty when we catch them and charge them, you'll have to."

She sighed in turn. "I know. I just don't like it." Her disgruntled tone had the two men hiding smiles even as Caleb continued his set up of the camera and Logan moved to where he was hidden from the camera but in her line of sight, knowing they were treading a fine line in his being there.

Caleb finally looked up at Aveleen, a prayer in his heart for her, as he watched her shift in her chair, her face white, her eyes dark with fear at what she had to remember. "Aveleen? All set."

She nodded, her eyes on him, consciously keeping them away from Logan, knowing if she looked at him, she could not and would not go through the coming statement.

Chapter 8

Licking nervously at her lips, her hands twisting together, Aveleen nodded as Caleb finished his instructions to her, her eyes on Logan for a moment, seeing his nod and smile of encouragement. She frowned for a moment as she saw that look again in his eyes, not sure what it meant, but she knew it was a look for her and her alone. She brought her gaze back to Caleb and sighed.

"We can't say we did and don't, can we?"

Caleb grinned at her, mirth sparkling for a moment past the concern on his face. "I wish we could. I would love nothing better than to not put you through this but we have no choice, Aveleen. We have to do this. The sooner we start, the sooner it's over." He paused, flicking a glance back at Logan before looking back at her. "When we're done, we need to talk. We need to put you somewhere safe."

"I'm not running, Caleb. Not again. I can't. I just don't have it in me." Her head dropped and the men watched as a single tear splashed off her hands, torn with wanting to end the matter but knowing she had to speak.

"Then, we'll send you somewhere on a vacation."

"I won't, I can't, go on my own and I won't ask anyone to go with me." She sighed, before raising her head and nodding. "Let's get this over with." Her words stopped as she once more bit at her lip, a habit Caleb noted that was new. This was not the self-confident Aveleen that he knew. He feared that person was gone for good.

Aveleen listened as Caleb started the tape, giving the location, names of those present and the date. He nodded to her.

She moistened her lips and began to speak, once more giving her full name and her date of birth and then the reason for her statement. She spoke rapidly at times but at other times, her words slowed and she fought to continue.

She thought back to where she had been when it had all started. She had just finished her work for the day, packing away her headphones she had been using as a transcriptionist for a law firm. She knew the law firm was part of another company but she had no contact with that company. In fact, she could not have said what the other company was or what they even did. She had risen from her desk, walking through to the kitchen in the building to wash and put away her cup, ready to face a weekend of fun as she thought ahead. Her brothers had wanted her to go to dinner with them, just the three of them. She had smiled as she thought of the fun they would have, just Aubrey, her older brother, and Avery, her younger one.

She turned as she heard a slight noise behind her, not expecting anyone else to be there. She had heard all the good nights as they left, leaving her alone in the building. She froze as she heard men's voices and then heard her own name. She spun, trying to find a hiding place but there was nothing. She ran for the door, heading through it towards the back door, knowing if she made it out she could find a place to hide. She barely heard the footsteps running towards her over the beating of her heart but felt the arms as they tightened around her, stopping her forward motion. She fought, struggling to escape but unable to. A hand across her mouth stopped her cries for help. She was forced through the back door and shoved into a vehicle, a hand clamped on her wrist preventing her from sliding across the seat and out the other door. She struggled, unable to escape the iron grip, before a gag was slapped over her mouth and then her hands bound.

She still struggled, before she felt a hand on her neck, holding her tightly and stopping her movements. She caught the barely audible words for her to stop fighting, that she would only hurt herself if she didn't. She frowned, the voice sounding familiar.

Darkness had fallen by the time they reached their destination. She searched, knowing the area. It was Cairn, her cousin, Holly's, hometown and a town she had spent a lot of time in during the summers as a child and teenager. The car crept through the town in the darkness, heading for the forest on the other side. Her heart dropped as she saw where they were headed. An old farmhouse, one that had been kept up, but not lived in for years, she knew from Holly. No one knew who the owner was or where they lived.

She was pulled from the car and showed towards the house, not allowed to stop or hesitate in any way. The two men with her kept too close an eye on her for her to even try to run. Inside the house, she was shoved up the stairs and into a bedroom, her bonds cut from her wrists, and then the door slammed and locked. She ran towards it, pulling on the knob, desperate to escape. She searched the room, looking for a way out. The windows were blacked out and she couldn't raise them. She finally sank to the floor in a corner, her head pillowed on her upraised knees, fear coursing through her at the unknown, her heart begging God to help her escape.

She finally crawled to the bed, exhausted in every point of her being, pulling the blanket off and covering herself as she lay on the floor, not willing to seek comfort. Her eyes open, she stared at the wall, seeing the fresh paint on it, and frowning. She really had no idea why she had been taken or who had taken her. Fear once more roused in her and she shook with absolute terror. Lord, please! Free me! Protect me! These words echoed through her mind and thoughts before she finally slept.

It was late the next morning before the door was unlocked and one of the men stood in the doorway before he motioned her to follow him. She shook her head and backed further away from him before a hand was on her arm and she was forcibly pulled from the room and down the stairs. She was shoved into a chair and a meal set in front of her that she refused to touch.

She finally reached for the sandwich, knowing she had to eat, but not sure if the food was drugged or not. When she was finished, the man appeared again, pointing to the stairs. She turned and ran for the door, clawing at the locks before she was forced away and up the stairs, no words spoken to her. She dropped to her knees as she heard the door slam and the lock click into place. She buried her face into her hands, praying for escape, but knowing it wouldn't be there.

Three weeks passed like this, before the day she was brought from her room, set down in the dining room. She frowned, knowing it was not meal time. She heard another set of footsteps behind her before they stopped, the man not coming around to face her.

"Where is the information on the company?"

She shook her head, not responding orally, waiting for what, she wasn't sure afterwards.

"The company? Where is it? Where is the information on it?" The voice was guttural enough that she was convinced he was disguising it.

"I don't know what you mean. What company?"

"You know which one." She could feel his breath on her head, he had moved in that close. "The one you were doing the letters on."

"I wasn't. I didn't do any letters for any company." She gave a low cry of pain as he grabbed a handful of her curls and twisted them, pain shooting through her scalp. "Please! Let me go!"

"Not until you give us the information that company. You know what we want."

"No, I don't." Anger laced her words. She gave a cry of pain and tears filled her eyes as he yanked her to her feet by her hair and shoved her towards another room, finally pushing her roughly into a chair. She blinked, seeing a laptop in front of her.

"Pull up your program."

She shook her head as best she could. "I can't. You can't access it anywhere but at the office."

Days passed before he appeared again. She had desperately tried to escape, to find an avenue she could flee but found nothing. Even when she made it to an outside door, it was locked, opening only with a key. She lost weight, fear, no terror, driving her to pace the floor at all hours. Sleep was fleeting at best.

She was shoved into the office one day, and down in the chair he always made her sit in. She wrapped her arms around herself, shivers running through her. How long had it been now? She had lost track of the days, with them rolling together in her mind. Her thoughts were no longer as clear as they should be. She was being beaten down and defeated. Her constant prayer for release was not answered and she had even begun to doubt that God really cared what happened to her. The Bible verses she drew from memory just didn't bring the comfort they should.

She stared at the desk top, not looking up. She had made that mistake one day and suffered for it. She jumped as arm reached in front of her and photos were placed on the desk. She drew a deep breath, shaky at best, and closed her eyes. Her family stared back at her. Her father, her mother, her two brothers - red ink slashing through their faces. No, she thought. Please, God. Not that. Keep them safe.

No words were said but none were needed. She shook her head, not able to provide what he wanted. She heard his footsteps walk away before she was shoved back up the stairs and the door to her room locked behind her. She sank to the floor, her back to the door, head buried on her knees. No tears came. She didn't think she had any left to cry.

The same scenario was repeated for a week, and then the photos changed to Holly and her husband. Aveleen again shook her head. She couldn't provide what they wanted.

He had finally given her the name of the company he wanted information on, BD Invests. She had replied that she didn't recognize the name. Didn't know the company or anyone who worked for it.

Two weeks later, she was once more shoved into the chair. This time, the photos staring back at her caused her to cry out with dismay. Her cousin, Hannah, and her husband, Caleb, and their children were pictured. She began to shake violently. He was threatening the police chief now. She didn't respond when he asked for the information he had been asking for all along. A hard blow sent her flying towards the floor, her face catching the corner of the desk as she fell. She gave a sharp cry of pain and laid still.

The man roughly shoved at her with his foot before using it to roll her over. He stared down at her dispassionately, a thunderous look on his face that she still refused to give him any information. He pointed at the blood on her face, instructing the men to deal with it. He was leaving and would be back in a few days. They had their orders.

Chapter 9

Aveleen roused slowly as she heard the footsteps approaching across the wood floor to where she slumped in a corner of the room.   She felt the hand on her arm, dragging her to her feet and then out of the room. No, Lord, please. No more. No more photos. I can't do this any more. She stumbled over her feet as she was roughly shoved down the stairs to the outside, tumbling to her hands and knees. The shock of the abrupt landing shook her. She raised her head and face to the sun, relishing its warmth in the early dawn, before she was shoved into a vehicle. She blinked rapidly, trying to keep her focus but too many days of stress, too little food, too little water had all taken a toll on her. Her head fell back against the seat and her eyes closed.

She didn't feel the rough shake she was being given or the curses that followed. She was pulled from the back seat of the vehicle and carried to the base of a cliff. She didn't know that the man who had placed her there on the ground stood back far enough so he could see up to the top of the cliff where his companion looked down at them, judging just where she had been laid, waving as he dropped a hat near the edge. She didn't hear the man move away, to stand in the shade of trees, his eyes watchful. She would have been horrified to know she was part of a trap, to catch an unwary opponent of the men's employer.

She didn't rouse as she felt gentle hands on her face and then her arms and legs, feeling for broken bones. She never felt the tenderness with which she was finally picked up in caring arms and taken from the spot. She roused at some point, just enough to see the dimness of the cave and feel the arms that held her close, the warmth of the man's arms holding her warming her. She spoke, but didn't really understand what she said or what he replied.

The next she knew she was waking in a bed, feeling clean and safe. She panicked, staring around, trying to determine just where she was and not able to. She jumped as she heard quiet footsteps and saw a woman she should recognize but couldn't. Her eyes slid shut again as a work-worn tender hand touched her face and called her by name.

She roused again, panic setting in, her movements causing the man seated beside her bed to stir and a hand come up to gently rest on her arm, stilling her panic and bringing her peace through his touch. She squinted through the dim light in the room, somehow recognizing him as the man who had saved her.

Aveleen was quiet for a moment, feeling as if she had told everything she could remember. She described the house in detail, the vehicles, the two men. She frowned, not able to give Caleb a description of their employer, but he just shook his head at her, motioning for her to continue.

She finally sat back, drained, her heart hurting, her head pounding, as Caleb stopped the video tape and reached for the bottle of water he handed to her, his other hand up to stop Logan from moving.

Caleb watched Aveleen closely, knowing how much it had taken from her, and fearing that the very act of giving her statement had set her back in her recovery. He didn't want Logan to approach her until he knew he had her complete statement. After handing her the bottle of water and watching closely as she drained it, he knew just how much it had taken for her to speak. His attention back on his laptop, he printed her statement, handing it to her.

"Read this over carefully, Aveleen, making any corrections and initialing and dating them. I think you spoke clearly enough that the speech program picked up your words."

Nodding slowly, her movements almost robot like, she took the pages and, propping her head on her hand, she read through, noting the changes needed and initialing as asked. She finally shoved the pages away, her eyes looking up at Caleb.

"Are we done, Caleb? Are we done? Do you need anything more?"

He shook his head, compassion on his face. "No. Not at this moment. I'll take this in and have the video tape transcribed as well." He shot a glance at Logan, finding him watching Aveleen intently. "We'll need to talk again, Aveleen. We need to keep at it until we catch these people."

"I was afraid that's what you would said." She sounded disgruntled, causing the men to bite back grins. She rose and headed away from them, shutting the bathroom door behind her and standing, hands gripping the edge of the vanity, staring at the whiteness of her face, the tired lines of exhaustion etched deep. Why, God, her heart whispered, too hurt and sore and tired to cry. Why did this happen to me? Where are You in this? I don't feel You near, not like I should. I know in my heart You are here with me, that You have not left me, but my head is saying You've gone, that I'm on my own.

Logan watched her walk away and then turned to Caleb, his question dying on his lips as he saw the look on Caleb's face.

"Caleb?"

Caleb shook himself and then looked over at Logan, finding the younger man with a puzzled look on his face. "Logan? She's hurting. I don't know if I've seen someone hurting like that. And I have seen a lot over the years. Not just on the job."

"I get that. But how do we help her?"

Caleb shrugged. "Right now, I am not sure what we can do to do just that. She's rejecting her life-long friends. I talked to her father. They desperately want to see her and I'm not sure if she'll even agree to that, not where she's at right now. Whatever was said to her, whatever the threats that were made against her family, she has buried it deep. I know she hasn't said everything. I know her well enough to know that she's hiding something."

"I am sure she is. I don't think she even realizes how deep she has shoved everything." Logan stood and began to pace. "How do we help her?"

"I am afraid we don't." He held up a hand as Logan spun and opened his mouth to speak. "It seems you are the only one who has been able to reach her. I know you're not working right now."

"But I am. I am doing guest columns for the paper I just left." Logan ran his hands through his hair. "I have a column due tomorrow, and I just can't concentrate on it." He spun, his eyes on the door behind which Aveleen had barricaded herself. "How do we help her?" He held up a hand.

"I know. I am repeating myself. If you can't help her, how do I?"

"I don't know, Logan. All I know is that you made a connection with her and brought her to safety. She's clinging to that." Caleb paused, his eyes watchful as he studied Logan and then shook his head. It's happening again, isn't it, Lord? He's fallen for her with a huge thud and just doesn't know what to do with it. He finally packed up his gear and left.

Logan stood on the porch of the cottage, studying the land surrounding the security compound Abe and his men called home. He could hear the calls and laughter of small children and the barking of dogs. He shook his head once more. Lord, how? How do I protect her? I'm not even sure from what. He reached for his laptop, bringing up a search engine and beginning his own search of the investment company. Then, sighing, he turned to his word processing program, knowing he had to do the promised column and not quite sure what to write on. This is one time You'll have to provide the words, Lord. I sure don't have them. Engrossed in his work, he didn't see or hear Aveleen pause in the doorway, her eyes on him, hope struggling against despair on her face as she let him into her heart and her life.

She finally turned, heading for the kitchen, a quick glance at the clock letting her know that time had flown that day. She quickly grabbed food and made his tea, reaching for a bottle of juice for herself, her hand pausing as she studied the bottle, a frown on her face. She didn't like orange juice, but here she was reaching for just that. She shrugged, thinking it odd but accepting that things had changed in her life, so maybe her food and beverage tastes had as well.

She hesitated as she shoved open the storm door with her hip and then approached the table in front of Logan, setting down the tray before standing, her hands running up and down her legs, an action she didn't even realize she was making.

Logan tensed for a moment, sensing someone in front of him, before he glanced up, a smile lighting his face as he saw Aveleen and then the tray of food. He set aside his work and rose, a hand reaching to draw her down onto the swing.

"Thank you, Aveleen. I was totally engrossed in my work." He asked a blessing on their food before motioning her to serve herself first.

She shook her head. "No, you first."

"Aveleen, let me explain something to you. I was raised that ladies are served first with a meal and then we men get ours. We don't expect to have you wait on us."

Aveleen's eyes were on his face, a thoughtful look crossing it. "That's how I was raised. I had forgotten." Tears sparkled for a moment. "What all did he take from me, Logan? And how do I get back to where I was?"

Chapter 10

A month later, Logan stood outside the newspaper office in Riverville. He had stood there many times but today he shoved open the door and entered. Caleb and Hannah had encouraged him to talk to the publisher but he had been reluctant to. Today, he was there on a mission to try and find information on the investment company. He had searched everywhere he could think of, finding nothing on the company. It was like it was a ghost. He paused, deep in thought, before he spun on his heel and headed back out the door, leaving the publisher staring after him before he shook his head.

Logan really had no idea where he was heading except he knew he wanted this over for his lady. He gave a small smile. That was how he thought of her. He had been back and forth between his hometown of Hope and Riverville, not content in either town, the desire to end Aveleen's terror and bring peace and comfort to her uppermost in his mind. They spent time together, but

Logan could see she did not feel safe. She still had not seen her family, although they had spoken. They had settled her into an apartment in the minister's garage and so far, she had been safe. He had chosen a house to rent not far from there.

He nodded at the townspeople he passed, stopping to speak with certain ones. They had accepted him into their church and their lives, making him feel as much as home as he could. He sighed. He really didn't like the unsettled feeling he had. Now he knew what Lincoln must have felt.

He paused in front of a store window, not seeing the books on display, before he moved on. He turned as he heard his name and saw Frankie running across the road towards him.

"Logan! Wait up a moment! You're just the person I need to talk to!"

"And why would that be?"

Frankie paused to catch his breath. "Deirdre has asked if you and Aveleen would like to come for a meal tonight? We're having a few friends over. Don't worry. Not a huge crowd." He sighed. "We are hoping that Aveleen will agree. Aubrey and Avery want to see her so desperately they're ready to do anything to get in touch. Her parents are the same, even though they understand why she's staying away from them."

Logan shook his head. "No, I don't think they understand just how it is with her." He frowned, turning in a circle as he felt eyes on him.

Frankie watched, comprehension dawning on his face. "The eyes?"

"What? The eyes?" Logan stopped, his eyes on Frankie's face. "Just what do you mean?"

"The eyes. You're being watched. You just can't pick out who it is."

"That's exactly it. Aveleen has said the same thing. She feels watched and has expected it. Neither of us like it."

Frankie grinned. "No, none of us did." He nodded. "Yep, Deirdre and I had what we term as an adventure." He sighed. "I think all our friends except for Caleb and Hannah did. But then Hannah used to tell Caleb who the culprit was."

"She didn't!" Logan wasn't sure that Frankie was not pulling his leg.

"She did. She nailed it with the ones after us." He turned, his eyes searching the area. "So, will you two come tonight?"

"Let me talk to Aveleen. It might help if you kept it small."

"Let me know. And we are planning on keeping it small. Caleb and Hannah. Dave and Rylee. Abe and Emma. Deirdre and myself. I want to bring in Aubrey and Avery, but only if she agrees."

"I'll talk to her and let you know." Logan watched Frankie walk away before he turned to the stores, searching for a particular one. He had a mission in mind and only one particular item would suffice.

Later that morning, Aveleen stared at Logan, her mouth opening and closing, even as she wrapped her arms around herself. "He wants what?"

"Frankie wants us to come for a meal. He also wants to bring in your brothers, in a safe place, just so you can talk."

She began to shake, causing Logan to reach for her and hug her tight. As always, she calmed, feeling the strength, peace and comfort he radiated to her. "I don't know, Logan. I really don't know. He's out there. He did threaten them."

"I know he did. But we have to live our lives, Sweetest." He leaned back. "I have to ask you something and this is something I have prayed long and hard about." He hesitated, seeing fear flicker across her face. "No, I am not walking away from you. I would never willingly do that."

She leaned against him again, her arms tightening around him. "I know you won't. It's just sometimes I think of how he threatened everyone who is close to me." She sighed. "I just wish I could remember exactly what he did threaten."

"It will come back to you, at some point. God knows when you will be ready for that. We'll just keep preparing for that eventuality."

She nodded. "Even when I get letters in the mail threatening me?"

He drew a deep breath. "Did you get a letter?" At her nod, he sighed to himself. "We can take it to Caleb tonight. No, I'm not pushing you to go. Just suggesting you need to get some of your life back. And I will be there every step of the way." He reached into his pocket and withdrew a box, opening to show her a gold cross. "I found this today for you. I would be honoured if you would accept it."

She stared at it and then at him, before she nodded, turning so he could fasten it. "Thank you, Logan." Her words choked off and she ran from him, leaving him staring after her, not sure what had happened.

The chiming of his phone drew his attention. Caleb was asking if they were coming. He sent a quick reply and then went to find Aveleen. She turned as he approached, a question on her face.

"Logan?"

"It's a gift to a wonderful lady and friend. I would like to explore our friendship, see where it ends. No strings at all, Aveleen. We'll work with how you are."

She nodded and then sighed. "Starting with tonight, you mean?"

He nodded. "It all depends on you. If you want to go, we can and just stay for a while. If you're not up to it, they're fine with it."

She sighed. "I know they are. It's just they went to all this trouble and I'm not sure how to feel."

"I will not leave your side, if that helps."

She stared at him. "You really mean that, don't you?" At his nod, she reached to hug him. "Thank you, Logan. All right. Just for a while. Do we need to take anything?"

He grinned. "Just you. That's all they want. Just to spend time with you. Frankie said he would send a message to your brothers to come only after you're there and we see how you are. They have agreed to that."

She snorted, bringing a laugh from him as they walked towards his car. "I can't see Aubrey or Avery agreeing to that. That's not them."

"They have. They are that concerned about you. They fully understand the risk they are running by coming near you." He shut the door after her, his hand resting for a moment on the car roof as he searched the area. I know, Lord. Someone is out there. Please, cover my lady with Your wings and hide her in the cleft of that rock. Protect her.

He slid behind the wheel, the key in the ignition before he turned to her. "I know what they are going through. Lincoln wouldn't have anything to do with either Larkin or I or our parents for a year. We didn't understand the gravity of what was going on. We lost a year together that we shouldn't have."

She studied him for a moment. "You really do get it from their point of view, don't you?" She turned to stare out the window. "I don't want them hurt, Logan."

He reached for her hand, giving it a quick squeeze even as he watched the vehicle behind him, making every turn and stop that he did. He turned quickly onto a side street and then into a parking lot, driving behind the stores and out of the other driveway, watching as the vehicle sped by and then made a quick u-turn to come back to the lot. He rapidly drove away, watchful, seeing Aveleen's questioning look before she leaned around to peer out the back window.

"What was that all about?"

"We had a tail. I just lost it."

"We did?" She slumped back on the seat. "It's him, isn't it? He's letting me know he's around."

"We don't know that for sure. I'll speak with Caleb tonight." He paused at a stop sign, then pulled through the intersection and to the side of the road. "If you want to go home, let me know. I'll take you home."

She studied him, seeing his sincerity before she sighed and then shook her head. "No. Let's go to where you promised I'd be."

"Are you sure? They will understand if you don't come. They've all been through stuff."

"I know. This isn't easy, you know."

"I know. I remember how it was with Lincoln and Holly, what they told me." He reached for her hands and bowed his head, bringing her before God, asking for peace and comfort for her.

She watched closely, panic beginning to set in as he parked at Frankie's place. It was out in the country, surrounded by trees, and that made her afraid. She finally slid from the seat as Logan held the door for her, and then studied her hand that he held tight in his as they walked up to where Frankie was waiting for them.

Frankie reached to hug Aveleen, eyes narrowing as she seemed to just tolerate a hug she would have freely returned before her captivity and watched as she moved closer to Logan, whose hand rested on her lower back. Logan gave a slight shake of his head and Frankie nodded. They would talk, he seemed to say, and later.

Chapter 11

Two hours later, Hannah approached the steps to the deck, her eyes on Aveleen as she sat on a lower one, Logan between her and the railing. She raised her eyes to Caleb and caught his quick nod. She sighed, not sure how they would proceed. Aubrey and Avery were here, out of sight of Aveleen, but where they could see their sister. She slid to a sitting position on the same step as Aveleen, watching her cousin closely, her eyes narrowing as she saw the necklace Aveleen was fingering.

She reached out a hand and stopped Aveleen's movements, studying the etching on the cross, before she raised her eyes to search Aveleen's face.

"I don't think I have ever seen you wear a cross before. You never wanted one." Hannah was puzzled.

"I know, Hannah. Things are different. I need this, right now." Aveleen shifted her weight, moving closer to Logan, who watched her face intently before he looked over her head at Hannah. "Logan gave it to me. He said he knew I needed it." She turned to watch her friend, a puzzled look on her face. "You never said why you knew that."

Logan shrugged, a slight smile on his face, tenderness in his eyes as he spoke. "God, Aveleen. I wasn't looking for a cross, but that's what I had to buy for you." He reached to tuck her hair behind her ear, his fingers lingering on the jagged scar in front of her ear, the caress drawing her face closer to his fingers.

Hannah nodded. "God knew. And He tells us these things. If we are open to Him and listen, that is."

Aveleen gave a small laugh. "And He has used you in ways He has not others." She rubbed her hand nervously on her jeans. "Hannah? What are you up to?"

Hannah reached for her cousin's hand. "Come, Deirdre has done some new plantings. She would like to have your opinion on them."

"No, please." She shrank back against Logan, his hand holding hers tightly.

"It's okay, Sweetest. I'll be right where you can see me and I'll come to you if you need me." Logan watched intently as she studied his face before she gave a reluctant nod and rose, walking down the yard with her cousin. He could tell she didn't want to do that, didn't want to leave him and the safety she felt with him, but she couldn't disappoint Hannah and Deirdre.

Logan finally rose and walked up the steps, his eyes searching for Aubrey and Avery, not seeing them, but knowing they were likely there somewhere. He took the mug of tea offered to him by Caleb and perched on the railing, one leg swinging, his mug resting on the railing beside him.

"How is she?" Caleb's quiet voice came through the talk and laughter around them.

"She's hurting, Caleb. She's so afraid." Logan looked down for a moment before he reached into his shirt pocket. He studied the envelope before he handed it over. "She got this today. I haven't looked at it. She said it was a threat but didn't say what."

Caleb tucked the envelope into a pocket. "I suspected that she'd get letters like this. Just watch for packages and tails."

Logan shook his head. "We had one tonight. I managed to lose it." He looked up as Caleb began to laugh. "You find that funny?"

"I do. It was one of my off-duty officers. He called, totally frustrated that you spotted him and that you were able to lose him. He searched for you, you know."

Logan grinned. "I should have stopped then? I didn't know."

"Now you do. But you did the right thing. He was quite impressed with how you lost him. He asked if you were joining the force. He volunteered to be your partner."

Logan laughed even as he shook his head, his eyes on Aveleen as she stood, arms wrapped around herself, talking with Hannah and Frankie's wife, Deirdre. "I'm not sure what I want to do, but joining the police force is definitely not me." He paused. "Her brothers are here?"

"They are. They've been watching her through the kitchen door, staying back so they can't be seen. Aubrey's fine with that. Avery, on the other hand, is angry." Caleb turned for a moment as he heard his name called. "I'll be right back, Logan. We need to go over strategy for the next few days."

Logan nodded, his thoughts drifting to the days and weeks ahead, knowing he had to make a decision on what he wanted to do with his life but feeling like he had to wait, Aveleen needing him. He didn't turn his head as he heard footsteps approaching, thinking it was Caleb returning. As the silence continued, he frowned and turned slightly, seeing two men standing there he didn't know.

The older one spoke. "You're Logan? You're the one who found Aveleen? Thank you."

"You must be Aubrey. And you're welcome. I just wish she'd talk with you."

"But she won't, will she?" Aubrey sighed. "Caleb and Hannah have both said she's changed."

"That's what I understand." He turned his head to watch her, seeing her moving away from Deirdre, towards a large bush. "She's been through stuff no one could even imagine."

Avery snorted. "That wouldn't change her. You did that."

Logan started to turn towards the younger man, even as he heard Aubrey's exclamation of his brother's name and the words to stop that torn from him before a fist connected with his jaw, snapping his head back, unbalancing him enough that he flew off the railing and dropped to the ground below, to lay in an awkward position, not moving.

Aveleen spun as she heard shouts and calls, seeing Aubrey tackle Avery and take him down on the deck, a puzzled look on her face for a moment before her eyes dropped to the ground below the deck and the men gathering there. She heard Hannah say Logan's name and she knew something had happened to him. She ran towards him, shoving her way past the men gathered there, dropping to her knees beside him, reaching for his hand, Dave on his knees on Logan's other side, assessing him, his voice calling for an ambulance. Aveleen felt hands on her arm, trying to draw her away and she flinched, the hands falling away as she did that. She heard voices around her but couldn't understand the words, her focus solely on Logan, knowing he was hurt and likely because of her, and that she had difficulty with.

She watched as Logan was loaded into an ambulance, Dave hopping up with him, the door slamming shut, blocking her sight on Logan. She began to shake, fear, no, terror, she thought, once more rising up within her. She heard Hannah's voice beside her before she was shoved into a vehicle and then Caleb was speeding after the ambulance. She didn't see her brothers standing staring after her, Aubrey concerned but saddened at what happened, Avery angry that she had not talked to them.

An hour later, Aveleen sat, her eyes fastened on the doors to the examination rooms, not speaking to the friends gathered around her. Hannah sat at her side, an arm linked through hers, feeling the stress, panic and terror rising in her cousin. She exchanged a look with Caleb, who sat on Aveleen's other side before he nodded and rose, heading to find the physician treating Logan.

Hannah tilted her head to stare past Aveleen, seeing Aveleen's parents and brothers hovering on the other side of the room, not sure if they should approach or not. Finally, Aveleen's mother, Meg, slipped into a chair beside her daughter, an arm coming around her, frowning as Aveleen ignored her. Hannah just shook her head at her aunt.

"Hannah? Where is Logan? Why won't he come out here?" Aveleen's voice was barely audible, the fear tracing through it breaking her cousin's heart. "He's left me, hasn't he?"

"Aveleen, he's been hurt. Remember? He was unconscious. Caleb's gone to see how he is."

"No, he's not there. He left. He's moved back to his hometown, hasn't he? Oh! What am I do to? I need to talk to him!" Tears thickened her voice, tears Hannah had never heard her cry before. "Oh, Hannah! What am I to do? I need to talk to him. I need to see him!" Panic was rising in her, and Hannah finally understood just how bad it was for Aveleen and how much she needed Logan in her life. "Hannah! I need Logan! Please! Help me find him!"

Meg watched, a frown still in place, as she listened to her daughter's words. This isn't right, she thought. She needs us, not some stranger. She spoke to Aveleen, who ignored her words.

Aveleen stood, intent on heading to the examination rooms but Hannah pulled her back down into a chair. Frankie stood nearby, watchful, knowing that this could be a moment when Aveleen was snatched from them again. He really didn't understand what had all happened to his friend, but he was not about to allow her to disappear again.

Hannah wrapped an arm around Aveleen, feeling the tension in her body, seeing her knees bouncing from the restless movement of her feet. She looked up as Caleb approaching, crouching down in front of Aveleen and reaching for her hands, taking a moment to compose himself at seeing her condition, his eyes raising to

Hannah. Hannah knew her husband was praying, it's what he did and who he was.

"Caleb? He's left, hasn't he? He's gone from here." Aveleen's voice was thick with tears, the terror and panic coming fighting through.

"No, he's still here, Aveleen. He's still unconscious." Caleb paused, his eyes seeing Meg watching closely, not saying anything even though she wanted to. He heard the footsteps approaching behind him and knew it was her father and brothers. "I can take you back. They've told me I can do that."

"You can? He's still here? He didn't leave me?" Hope struggled with despair as she took in his words. "He's hurt? Who did that to him? I thought he fell."

"No, he didn't fall on his own. He was hit." Caleb heard Meg's indrawn breath and realized she hadn't know that.

"Who did that? Who hit my Logan?" Anger sparked in her, something none of them had ever seen in her.

Aubrey spoke. "Avery sucker punched him, Aveleen, before I could stop him."

Meg and Michael stared at their youngest son, horrified that he had done that. Before anyone could say anything else, Aveleen was on her feet, anger on her face as she stared up at her younger brother before her hand was raised and she struck him across the face, causing his head to fly to the side, a red mark appearing on his cheek as he raised his own hand to his face.

"I hate you, Avery. I don't want to see you. Ever again." She turned to Caleb, tears on her cheeks. "Caleb? Please? Logan? You said I could see him."

"And that you can. Come." His arm around her, he drew her away from the group, not looking back.

Meg stared at her youngest son. "Avery? You did that? You hurt a man? How could you?"

"He's taking her away from us. That's why!"

Michael drew his family away from the crowd, Hannah with them, Frankie and Dave following. "Enough already. Avery, that was wrong of you. From what I understand, Logan is the only one who can reach through whatever it is that your sister is feeling and help her.   Did you not understand that?"

Avery shook his head, anger still on his face. "We can do that too, Dad."

"No, we can't. Not in that way. You saw her. She needs him in a way we can't help her."   Michael paused, his eyes sorrowful as he watched his daughter walk away from her family, seeking comfort from the only one she knew could bring it. "You will apologize when you see her next. And keep apologizing.   And spend hours in prayer. You need to seek forgiveness for both of them and from God." He turned at a movement from Aubrey. "Aubrey?"

"He'll need to grovel, Dad, and grovel well. That's where she's at. An apology just won't do."

Michael bit back a smile even as Meg shook her finger at her sons.

"Listen to me, you both. You may have just drove her from her family, Avery. Please? Do what you can to make it right?" Tears sparkled on her cheeks as she turned, Hannah's arm around her as she led her back to a seat.

Chapter 12

His arm still around her supporting her, Caleb paused at the cubicle where Logan had been. He knew they had planned to take him for imaging and X-rays but he had hoped he would be returned there by now. This is not what Aveleen needed, not with the state she was in.

"Caleb? He's not here. You said he was. Oh! He's gone already, isn't he? He really has left. What am I to do?"

"It's okay, Aveleen. He'll be right back. They needed to do some X-rays. He won't leave you. I know that for a fact." He looked around as he heard wheels heading their way. "Here. He's back. Let them get him settled back in the cubicle and then we'll go in."

She spun at his words, her hands covering her mouth, her eyes huge as she saw Logan, relief that he really was there coursing through her body, causing her to lean harder on Caleb. "He really didn't leave, did he? Caleb, what am I to do? I can't depend on anyone this way. It's too hard."

"Ssh, Aveleen. It's okay. Logan understands you need him. He needs you." Caleb finally let her go and watched her approach carefully to where Logan lay on the stretcher, his eyes closed.

Aveleen's hands ached to hold onto Logan's but she wasn't sure if she could or even should. Finally, she reached a tentative hand to his and held tight, feeling his fingers tighten on hers. His eyes stayed closed but she felt the comfort flowing to her that she always felt around him. She relaxed, her eyes studying him, before she looked up and around the room.

Caleb watched closely as she finally just stood, her head bowed. He turned as he heard footsteps and Frankie stood beside him, his eyes assessed the couple in the room.

"How is he?"

"I haven't heard yet. I put in a call to Lincoln, and he's to call the physician. I'll speak with him at some point."

Frankie nodded towards Aveleen. "How's Aveleen? That was intense in the waiting room."

"It was. I didn't think she had that much anger in her or that she would ever react like that. She wouldn't have before this all started." Caleb turned slightly as he heard his name. "Doc? What can you tell me?"

The physician stopped, his eyes too finding Aveleen and Logan. "That's his lady?"

"It appears so." Frankie turned as he felt watched, not seeing anyone that he didn't recognize. "Someone's watching them, Caleb."

"I know. I just don't know who." Caleb turned back to the physician. "Doc?"

"I spoke with his brother and he okayed me talking to you, although he didn't need to. Just a precaution, given that Hannah's involved in this." The physician studied Aveleen. "She really isn't doing well, is she?"

"Not really. She's changed. The only one who can calm her or get through to her

is Logan. And right now, he can't do that."
Caleb turned once more, a frown on his face.
"How is he?"

"Nothing broken. I can't confirm a concussion as yet, but he may have one. Heavy bruising on the jaw. But you knew that already." He shook his head. "Considering how far you say he fell, he's fortunate. I would say he was unconscious when he hit the ground and that may have saved him from further injury." He walked away, leaving Caleb nodding even as he turned back to Frankie.

Frankie watched for a moment before he excused himself, saying they would drive Hannah home. Caleb nodded, knowing he wouldn't be leaving, not for a while any way. He heard footsteps stop beside him.

"How is he, Caleb?" Michael had found him.

"Lucky, I would say. Nothing broken. No concussion. If he would wake up, Aveleen would be better." He nodded towards Aveleen. "We won't get her to leave him. He's the only one who can calm her, even unconscious as he is. She changed as soon as she took his hand."

"She did? Their bond is that strong?" Michael shook his head. "I guess we didn't understand. I have never seen anyone in a state such as Aveleen was in."

"That was mild. The day she came back to town, she was in a full-blown panic. In all my years in law enforcement, I don't think I have seen anyone that bad."

"What has caused it, Caleb? Do you know?" Michael watched as Aveleen turned, seeing him, her heart in her eyes as she walked towards him and into his hug. His arms tightened around his only daughter, as tears blinded him.

"Fear. Terror. Only Aveleen can tell us for sure, and she's not able to do that." Caleb watched with compassion as Aveleen nodded against her father.

"I'm sorry, Dad. I don't know why I feel like this."

"I understand now, Aveleen. Aubrey got it, I think, before any of us. Avery will take time." He smiled. "Your mother lit into him, you know."

"He shouldn't have done that, Dad. Logan didn't do anything to him."

"No. The only thing Logan did was step in and protect you and be your friend. He's been the support that Avery wants to be and can't." He sighed. "You'll have to apologize to him, you know."

"I will, at some point. I'm just not sorry I did that. He's had it coming for a long time."

Michael froze in his movements, not quite sure what she meant. "What do you mean, love?"

She shrugged. "He's too protective. I was planning on moving away from here, just to get away from him. He's made my life miserable."

"Oh, love, why didn't you talk to us?"

"It wouldn't have made any difference, Dad. You and Mom would have just told us to work it out. With Avery, that means it's his way. He doesn't listen very well. Aubrey supported me, was willing to help me find a new town, a new job, a new life. He wanted to talk to you and Mom but I wouldn't let him."

"Oh, love. How I wish you had! Let me talk to Avery."

"No one can get through to him, Dad. You've tried over the years." She stepped back, swiping at the tears on her face, leaving her father shocked at the sight of them. "I need to get back to Logan." She turned and almost ran from them.

"Did you know that, Caleb?"

"Not really, Michael. I suspected something. Hannah had warned me something was going on with those two, but she wasn't even sure what."

"With what's going on now, how do we reach her and convince her to stay?" Michael began to pace, distraught at his daughter's words.

"Leave it with God, Michael. That's all you can do. You can talk to Avery, but I don't think you'll get through to him. He's too angry right now."

"He is and he has been, now that you mention it. We've noticed a change in him and couldn't figure out why. Did he suspect or know Aveleen's plans?"

Caleb watched as Aveleen pulled a chair over to the stretcher, dropping into it, her hand reaching for Logan's. "We need

Logan up and on his feet. He's the only one I've seen calm her."

Michael nodded, then sighed. "I need to go have a family meeting by the sounds of it. Call me, Caleb, as soon as Logan wakes up, if you're still here. I want to talk to him as soon as I can. I need him to stay in Aveleen's life and right now I'm not sure he will."

"Trust me, Michael, he's going nowhere. That's a given. Unless Aveleen sends him away, he's in her life for the long run."

"I'm glad. I need to get to know him." Michael hesitated before he shook his head and walked away.

Caleb watched him go, turning as he heard wheels approaching and stepped out of the way of the cleaning cart, a frown on his face. The man seemed familiar but he wasn't sure and that was unusual for him. He studied the heavy gray beard and hair, the stooped posture and shook his head. No, it wasn't him, but it had to be a relative. He opened his mouth to speak when he heard Aveleen speak.

He walked towards her, standing beside as she spoke to Logan, the sound of her quiet voice stilling his restless movements. He watched as she raised her eyes to study the room and the equipment before she seemed to freeze in place, fear in her very being.

"He's here, Caleb. Out in the hallway somewhere. He's here. He's watching me." The panic began to rise within her.

Logan's hand tightened on hers as he moved restlessly, knowing even as he was rousing that he needed to calm her. His first conscious thought was a prayer for his lady, that God would protect her and bring her the peace she needed. A groan was torn from him and he felt her hand slip from his and then gently touch his face before his vision darkened again and he slipped away from her.

Aveleen bit at her lips, desperate to stem the flow of tears once more. She felt Caleb's arm around her shoulders and heard his prayers for both Logan and herself, but she felt so far away from God, she doubted He heard her heart anyway.

Chapter 13

A month had passed since Avery's assault on Logan. Logan had healed physically but emotionally he was torn. He saw the devastation in his lady that the assault had brought, saw the fracture in the family, saw how Aveleen went out of her way to avoid her parents and Avery. Aubrey she could tolerate but didn't go around him for long periods of time. This broke Logan's heart, knowing how he had felt when Lincoln had chosen to stay away from his own family. He had tried to reason with her but she had just stared at him, shrugged, and walked away. He spent hours in prayer for her, knowing that was all he could do.

He turned from his desk in the house he had purchased in town, knowing he would never walk away from his lady. He rose, heading for the door, seeing through the front window the police cruiser sitting in his driveway. He sighed. This is not what he needed. His columns were growing in popularity and editors from a number of newspapers were contacting him. He had more work almost than he could handle.

Frankie turned to face him as he opened the door, holding up a file. "We need to talk, Logan. Caleb sent me."

Logan stepped back and headed for the kitchen, knowing Frankie would welcome a mug of coffee. He made the coffee for Frankie and then tea for himself before he pointed to the back door.

"What do you have?"

"Aveleen didn't tell you about all the letters and parcels she's been getting?"

Logan paused as he sipped at his tea, before he shook his head. "No, she hasn't but that doesn't surprise me. She's trying to not worry me and that makes it worse. I can't force her to tell me. I don't have that right."

"They're getting more and more vicious, Logan. They have started to threaten you again." Frankie handed over the folder. "Caleb authorized me to give you some of them, but not all. Read through them. See what you make of it." He gave a quick grin. "Just don't go investigating on your own."

Logan snorted. "Now that you've told me that, it's like telling the sun not to rise." He stared towards the trees surrounding his house, knowing he should have chosen a different one, with more open ground around it. Aveleen at times was uncomfortable being there.

"You need to talk to her. See if she'll open up to you and tell you if she's remembered anything. She's refusing to talk to Caleb or myself. It's to the point we may need to bring in someone from outside to talk to her and that won't go over well."

"Who would you bring in?" Logan held up a hand. "No, don't tell me. Don't go that route yet. Let me talk with her."

Frankie nodded, finished his coffee and turned for the door. "You should just marry her, Logan. Your feelings are there for everyone to see." He walked away, leaving Logan staring after him.

"He's right, Lord. My feelings are out there, aren't they? I guess I need to talk to her, but the timing isn't right. Not yet. She just needs a friend, not pressure for something more."

Logan finally pushed away from his desk once more, squinting at the clock. Late afternoon, and he was to pick Aveleen up for a date in thirty minutes. He would need to rush and he hated rushing when he was heading to meet her. He stared at his computer screen for a moment, seeing the name he had chosen for his columns - The Pioneer. He had no idea where that came from, but God was leading him to use his columns to spread His word and work. That was what he had been missing before.

Aveleen stood in the entry of the restaurant, her face pale, unable to move her feet forward to head for the table that Logan had reserved for them. He watched her closely before he beckoned the waitress back, handing her a tip and then, hand on Aveleen's back, turned her around and moved her back out the door and to his car. He shut the door after she was seated, his eyes on her face, seeing the look that broke his heart. That look had been absent for a few days and hope had begun to rise that maybe the culprit had moved on.

He slid behind the wheel, not starting the vehicle, and twisted in his seat to watch his lady, seeing the emotions simmering just below the surface.

"Aveleen? What did you get today?"

She jumped, his voice startling her. "How did you know I got something?"

"It shows on your face and in your movements." He sighed, knowing he would have to confess. "Frankie was by earlier today. Caleb sent some documents to me."

"He wasn't supposed to. I asked him not to." She wrapped her arms tightly around herself, not looking at him.

"The ones he sent were interesting. I wish you had talked to me. I would rather hear from you than him." He reached out for her hand, holding it tightly in his. "Aveleen, look at me. Please?" He waited until she did, his heart breaking at the tears glistening in her eyes.

"Logan. Please. I don't want you hurt. It was bad enough what Avery did to you." She stopped, biting at her lips, the expression on his face bringing a halt to her words.

"Aveleen, Sweetest, I am going nowhere. I can't walk away from you. Not today. Not ever. I love you too much to do that. Please? Let me stay in your life."

She stared at him, her hand to her mouth, as she took in his words. "Logan, I have brought you nothing but trouble. First, you're kidnapped. Then you move from your hometown. I get constant threats directed towards myself, you, your family, my family. And then Avery hit you so hard. I thought I had lost you that night, Logan." She paused, her face turning to the front. "I didn't know you loved me."

"I do, more than my own life, right below my love for God. I love you more than my own family. I want to live the rest of my life with you, for however long we're granted. But you need time. Time was taken from you and you're just now starting to see that it wasn't you."

She shook her head, her eyes coming back to him, searching his face, seeing his heart in his eyes. "Logan, what am I do to with you? You are the only one who can calm me, make me feel safe and secure. You're my rock. How am I to live without you?" She paused, a slight smile on her face. "You're not going to ask, are you?"

"Ask what?" He gave a small grin, knowing exactly what she was saying.

"You won't ask me to marry you, because you think it's too soon. I don't." She bit at her lip again, her hand tightening on his. "I'm going to be bold, Logan, and you know me well enough to know I'm not bold. I never have been. People think I'm so confident and settled. This has shown me that I wasn't as secure in God as I should have been. I have doubted Him."

"It's only human to do that, Sweetest. God understands."

"I know. It's still feels wrong." She looked down at their hands. "Logan, will you marry me? Grow old with me?" She waited, finally looking up with a sinking heart when he didn't answer.

Logan was unable to speak, knowing just what it had taken for her to ask him that. He nodded, his free hand reaching to touch her face. "I will." His words were barely a whisper. "I will, Sweetest."

She sighed, a softened look on her face. "Thank you."

Logan walked her to her door later that night, reaching to envelope her in a hug, bending to kiss the scar on her cheek before he kissed her good night. She stood, her eyes on him, before she turned, locking the door behind her, resting her back against it.

Lord, what did I just go and do? I just asked him to marry me. That should have been his place. She sank to the floor, her head on her knees as sobs shook her body. She didn't know why she was weeping, only that she had to.

Logan listened to the sobs as he stood, head bowed, hand flat on the door. He wanted to break the door down to reach her but knew he had to walk away, had to let her have this time.

He paused as he reached his car, his hand on the door, a frown on his face as he saw the envelope under the wiper blade. His hand on it, he waited, looking around, feeling the eyes on him. He opened it, a stern look crossing his face. He needed this to end, he thought. Aveleen didn't need to be threatened every day with death. He looked back down at the paper. That was exactly what they had threatened. He slid into his car, heading for Caleb, then turned towards his own home. He needed to pray this through before he talked to Frankie, he decided. Caleb was too close.

He pulled to a stop in his driveway, heading into his house and changing from his good clothes to jeans and a sweatshirt. He grabbed the backpack he always kept ready and headed back to Aveleen, parking across from her house and planning on spending the night. He was too afraid for her to do anything else.

Chapter 14

Logan walked towards the police department two weeks later. He was frustrated. No one had been able to track the letter he had received that night. And Frankie admitted they were getting nowhere in their search for her abductors. The company name had been ruled as wrong and she could give no other name. She wasn't even sure that was the name.

He had pulled out his investigative tools and tried his best to search but he too had reached a dead end. And he didn't like that. He knew God was watching over them, that he needed to rely on Him but he still hurt for his lady. She had not said much to him over the last few weeks, but he knew it was weighing her down. He could see it in her eyes when she didn't think he was watching.

He spun on his heel, heading back the way he had just walked, not seeing the man he had almost ran into turn and follow him. His thoughts were on Aveleen and he needed to see her.

Aveleen stood in her kitchen, her eyes huge, as she listened to Logan.

"Logan, we can't just do that!"

"We can. I think we need to. You've already asked me to marry you." He held out his left hand, wiggling his ring finger, a grin on his face. "Okay. So, where's my ring?"

"Logan!" Her cry of outrage was enough for him to cross the room and envelope her into his arms.

"I know, Aveleen. This is not how you imagined getting married. We can make our marriage a lifelong courtship. But I will not push you. It's your decision. Enough has been taken from you over the last year." He turned his head as he heard the doorbell. "Were you expecting anyone?"

"No! It's become a bus station around here today. First Aubrey, then you, and now whoever it is at the door. Please? Get rid of them." She moved away to stand with her back to him, staring out the kitchen window, listening as his footsteps faded.

She heard him return and stop just inside the kitchen door without saying a word. She finally spoke.

"Well? Did whoever it was leave?" When he didn't respond, she spun, her face flushing as she saw Greg Evans, her minister, standing there, a grin on his face. "Greg! I'm sorry. I didn't know it was you."

"Obviously not. It's okay, Aveleen. I've had worse welcomes than yours." He looked between the two of them. "Now, tell me why I'm here?"

"What? What do you mean?" Aveleen stared at Logan, who just shrugged.

"God told me I had to come right now to see you two. Why?" He held up a hand. "Can we sit? I have a feeling it's going to be a long discussion."

Logan shook his head. "I have no idea. Why would God send you here?"

Greg held up a hand. "First, let me pray for you two. You've been through a lot, Aveleen. And it's far from over." When he had finished, he looked between the two. "So, what are you two planning?"

Logan shared a look with Aveleen and grinned at the mutinous look on her face. "It's like this. Aveleen asked me to marry her, and we're trying to work through that."

Greg choked on the water in his mouth, coughing when he finally swallowed it. "Aveleen? Aveleen asked you to marry her? I doubt that. It's not her." He paused, his eyes tracing between the two. "I'm sorry, Aveleen. I spoke out of turn. That's not the you we knew before. Now, I can see that. Whatever you went through uncovered depths no one ever knew you had."

"It did?" Aveleen sat back, her eyes on her folded hands. "I don't like the person I've become, Greg."

Logan's hand covered hers. "I didn't know you before, Aveleen, but I admire the courageous, resourceful woman you have become. It wasn't your choice, but God has been with you through everything. He has plumbed the depths of your character and tried you in fire, bringing forth a beautiful wonderful woman that I love deeply. Sweetest, I wouldn't change you back."

She had looked up at him as he began to speak, a puzzled look on her face.

Ignoring Greg's watchful eyes, she spoke. "Logan? What's with that word?"

"What word?" He shook his head. "I'm not sure what you mean."

"Sweetest. You call me Sweetest all the time. Why? It's not a term of endearment. Not that I am aware of."

He raised her hand and kissed the back of it. "Sweetest? That word? It's part of a phrase. I wasn't sure you were ready to hear it. Sweetest - it's a short form for the phrase that you're the sweetest thing in my life and always well be."

Her face softened as he spoke. "Thank you, Logan. Do you know how much I needed to hear that?"

"I know, Aveleen. I do know." He looked over at Greg. "Now, why would Greg be here when neither of us called him?"

"He said God told him to come." Aveleen turned her attention to him. "Greg?"

Greg had been listening with interest to Logan's explanation before he looked over at Aveleen. "Is it true?"

"Is what true?"

"Did you really ask him to marry you?" He grinned as she groaned and hid her face. "I take it that's a yes."

"I did but only because he wasn't going to ask. He thought I needed more time."

"And do you?"

She shrugged, her eyes finding Logan and seeing the love he felt for her on his face. "I don't know, Greg, to be honest. I really don't know. We were talking about that when you came."

"Then that's why I'm here. God knew you needed me at this particular time and place." He sat back, his face thoughtful as he stared across the room. "What are your objections to getting married right now? Have you talked through what you want and where you want to go?"

The young couple shook their heads.

"We haven't really thought about it. At least I haven't." Aveleen's confession was barely audible. "But I don't want to lose Logan if I say I need time."

"I doubt that will happen, Aveleen. He's talked to me." Her eyes shot up to him and then to Logan, who nodded.

"I have, Aveleen. Given what you've been through, I needed some advice. I didn't want to put you on the spot and have you regret saying yes." He looked down, swallowing hard. His voice was broken as he continued. "I just needed to talk to someone who knew you. That's all."

Her hand tightened on his. "Thank you, Logan. You always put others ahead of yourself." She looked over at Greg. "Greg?"

He nodded. "He does, Aveleen. I've seen that. Others have commented on it. I have also been told he is perfect for you, that he draws you out from where you have hidden yourself." He smiled, his eyes compassionate as she shook for a moment. "It's true. You have hidden yourself away because of what you've gone through. We understand you need time. And that time is what God has planned for you. I know you're far from finished with your abductor. That's a given."

"I know and I am so afraid." Her voice was barely a whisper. "I don't want Logan hurt. That's why I won't commit to a date."

"But if you knew you only had a few weeks, a few months, what would you say? Would you risk losing that time together to fear?" Greg paused. "God knows your hearts, you two. He has put you together at this time. You need to trust, and I get it that's a difficult thing for you to do." He reached into his shirt pocket, pulling out his pocket Bible. "Let's work through this, okay?"

"But, Greg, you don't have time. It's your men's meeting tonight." Aveleen grew agitated at the thought of him missing that.

"No. Tonight, I have you two. You're more important. One of the deacons has stepped in for me. And no, they don't know I'm here. I just asked them to pray for a situation I became aware of and that I felt God wanted me to be there for the people involved. You know our church, Aveleen. We don't need specifics to pray. We just need to be asked."

Greg led them from passage of Scripture to passage of Scripture about trust, about fear, about marriage, taking time to listen to them, responding to their questions, and finally sitting back, letting them absorb his words and what God had said.

"Aveleen?" Logan's voice was quiet. "What are your thoughts?"

She shrugged. "I'm still not sure, Logan. I need to pray about this." She looked up at the ceiling, tears blinding her for a moment as she bit at her lip. "I am just so afraid."

"Then, we wait. We wait until you've had time." Logan looked over at Greg who was nodding. "We don't rush. You've had such an upset in your life and it's turned everything you know and trust upside down."

"Thank you, Greg." She rose and almost ran from the room, sobs shaking her body.

The two men rose as well and stood outside talking before Greg headed off. Logan looked back at the house and then seated himself on the steps. He would wait, he decided, until she was ready. All teasing

aside, he wouldn't push her. He didn't see
the vehicle parked across the street, or the
open window with traces of cigarette smoke
rising into the air through it. He didn't see
the man finally toss the cigarette butt out the
window and then drive off. Perhaps, if he
had, things might have been different in the
future.

Chapter 15

Aveleen turned in a circle in her yard, watching the birds take flight. Something had startled them and she was suddenly afraid. She ran for her home, slamming the door and shoving home the locks on the back door and flying for the front door to do the same. A prisoner, she thought. I am a prisoner. Still. And in my own home. Lord, when will it end? When will I be able to live my life without looking over my shoulder?

She almost ran for the room she had set up as an office and slid into a chair, her eyes on her computer as she pulled up her internet program and began a search. Something was niggling at her mind, a name that she just could not bring to the forefront. She became her own search for the investment company, her fingers pausing as she read a name, fear suddenly striking through her. She shoved back from her desk, tumbling from her chair, her hands clamped over her mouth before she ran from the room, from the house, and towards the road.

Logan had been heading her way, intent on asking her to go somewhere with him. He watched as she ran towards him, tears on her cheeks. He slid from his vehicle, arms open to welcome her, holding her tight as she sobbed.

His voice finally reached through the terror she felt and she tilted her head back to look up at him.

"Aveleen? What happened?"

"I think I found the name, Logan. Or at least one of the names. And he's from here. I've known him all my life." She continued to shake with fear.

He shoved her into his car, locking the doors and heading for her home, searching through the rooms, until he stood looking at her computer screen, reading the text. He reached to print it, knowing it was needed to be taken to Caleb. Locking up after himself, he stood for a moment, feeling the eyes watching him. He didn't like that one bit. He knew he would be pushing Aveleen to make a decision. He wanted her with him all the time, wanted to protect her with his life if necessary, but he knew she needed to be the one making that decision.

Caleb reached for the papers that Logan extended to him, his keen eyes assessing Logan.

"Where's Aveleen?"

"Locked in my car. I just wanted to hand you that. She recognized the name as one of the men who held her captive. I'm leaving it with you. We're disappearing for a while. Call Lincoln if you need to reach me. He'll be the only one who knows where I am."

"Logan! Wait! That's not a good idea." Caleb walked through the entry doors to the police department, searching the area before he trained his sight on Aveleen. He was shocked at the whiteness of her face, the devastation he saw there. "Are you sure?"

"I am. I have no idea where we're heading, but it's away from here."

Caleb's hand on his arm stopped him. "Just a moment. You have no idea where to go. Let me talk to Abe. Ian can fly you two somewhere."

Logan shook his head. "That puts more people at risk. Aveleen doesn't want that. Nor do I." Logan shook off Caleb's hand and ran for the car, pulling away from the curb, carefully watching for a tail and not seeing anyone.

"Where are we heading, Logan?" Aveleen's voice was quiet, almost too quiet, he thought.

"I really don't know. First, Aveleen, we need to make a decision. We can't go away on our own as an unmarried couple. You do understand that?"

She nodded, knowing he was thinking ahead to the talk that would be sure to follow them. She sighed, reaching to brush away a tear before she reached for his hand. "Do we see Greg?"

He shook his head. "No. That's what everyone would expect us to do. Greg mentioned that he has a friend in a neighbouring town and recommended we see him. I gave him the okay to talk to him." He suddenly gave a laugh, startling her. "Apparently he has quite a story as well. He married his wife quickly to protect her."

"He did? What is it with people today? Don't they do anything the old-fashioned way?"

"I guess not. It's just your friends seem to attract trouble."

Logan headed away from Riverville, his heart heavy for his lady. He had no idea where they were going, where they would end up, or even when she could come back to her hometown and her family. He didn't like the feeling he had that they were just starting out on a journey that could mean the death of one of them. His heart cried out to God, asking for protection for his lady. His own life didn't count, he thought, not realizing that he would come so close to losing not only his own life but his lady as well.

He pulled to a stop in front of a house and stared at it, liking the homey atmosphere and comfort and peace it emanated. He reached for Aveleen's hand, not liking the cold fingers he grasped tightly.

"Aveleen, I won't force this. If you say no, you're not ready to get married, we'll figure out something."

She nodded, a somber look on her face. "I know you will, Logan. I also know you have prayed long and hard about this. I have too. It's just not what I wanted."

He kissed her, and leaned his forehead against her temple. "I know, Sweetest. I know. It hurts." He jumped as he heard a tap on his window and spun in his seat, staring at the tall man standing there, a large smile on his face. He hit the window button and frowned at the young woman standing there as well.

"Greg said you were heading this way at some point. He described you and your car well. You must be Logan and Aveleen."

"We are." Logan shoved open the door and then hurried around to open Aveleen's door, helping her out and tucking her tight against him, feeling her calming down at his touch.

"I'm Silas Peters and this is my wife, Madigan. Come on in. Madi has a meal ready for us."

Logan finally sat back, resting an arm along Aveleen's shoulders as he talked with Silas, listening to Madigan talk gently with Aveleen, drawing her out, before she rose and took Aveleen with her to the backyard, the twilight bringing a welcome cooling.

Silas watched as the two women walked away before he turned to Logan.

"Logan? Where does the investigation stand? Do you know?"

Logan shook his head. "Not where I would like it to be. Aveleen just remembered the name of one of the men who held her today. I gave that information to Caleb, but he'll need to work with it before he can make a case. He has no idea how long that will take." His words stopped as he thought through the time facing them. "How do we do it, Silas? How do we go on with our lives, with this hanging over us?"

"Have you talked to your brother?"

"I have. He was no help." Silas grinned at the disgruntled tone in Logan's voice. "He just says God got them through." Logan sighed, knowing he was feeling out of sorts. "How do I do that to Aveleen, Silas? How do I marry her with this hanging over us? She may change her mind."

"I don't think she will. She's deeply in love with you, just watching her shows that. And you are with her. You both also have a deep love for God. He's first in your lives and that's how it should be." Silas went on to describe how God had worked it out for Madigan and himself.

Logan sat back. "A dead body in the church? Oh my! How do you go back in there every day?"

"By God's grace. I must say, some days are difficult." He turned as he heard a tap at the door and frowned. "Stay put. I'll be right back."

Silas returned, a slight smile on his face. "Greg has tracked you down."

"He has? That's not good."

Silas shook his head, his smile deepening. "No one will know this is for you." He handed over the envelope. He poked at it as Logan stared first at him and then down at the envelope. "I suspect it's the documentation you two need." He rose, heading for the door. "Madi? Can you and Aveleen come on in? Greg's sent something for Logan and Aveleen."

Aveleen handled the envelope with great care before she dropped it, her eyes on Logan. "What would he have sent us?"

"I have no idea." Logan reached for the envelope, hesitating a moment as a shudder of fear ran through him. "I don't like this, Aveleen."

"I don't either." She watched as he carefully opened the larger envelope, shaking out smaller ones and some photos. "What is this?"

Logan sorted through the pile of papers, setting the envelopes aside as he turned his attention to the photos, drawing in a deep breath as he did so. "It's our homes, Aveleen. These are crime scene photos."

"Crime scene?" Her voice rose to a higher pitch before she wrapped her arms around herself and began to shake. "What do you mean? Crime scene photos? And how do you know that's what they are?"

"The police tape is a giveaway for one thing." He looked up abruptly, sharing a look with Silas, who nodded. "It appears someone has broken into our homes. I am just so glad you weren't there."

"Did Caleb send those?"

"No, Frankie got these to Greg. And Greg sent them on to us. It's a warning, Aveleen. We can't go home now. They're really getting desperate to find you."

She nodded, her hand reaching for an envelope with her name on it. She hesitated before she opened it. "It's from my parents. They want to talk to us, Logan. They want to see us too. I can't do that. Not now."

His arm around her, he rested his head against her, ignoring Silas and Madigan. "We won't go near them. Not unless we need to. The same for Lincoln and Holly. We can't put them at risk." He sighed, his head tilting back as he looked to the ceiling for answers. "Where will it end, Aveleen?"

"With me dead, I think. I couldn't help them. Now they need to punish me." She looked at him. "Greg was right."

"He was? About what?"

"We can't live in fear, waiting for better times. God doesn't want that for us. He wants us to be the people He is making us into, to be free to share Him with others. If we're hiding and living in fear, we can't do that."

"Are you saying what I think you're saying?" He waited, almost not breathing, hope rising within him.

She studied him for a long moment before she nodded. "I am, Logan. I think we need to take the next step. I have peace that's where God is leading us."

He studied her for a moment, then sat back, a frown on his face. Was it really what God wanted, he wondered? Or was it something he was pushing for, just because he was afraid he would lose her.

Silas was watching Logan's face, a frown in place even as he felt Madigan's hand on his arm.

"Logan? What are your thoughts?" Silas' voice broke through the thoughts swirling in Logan's brain.

Logan shook his head and then abruptly pushed back from the table, heading for the outdoors, leaving Aveleen staring after him, a bereft look on her face, her hands over her mouth. Silas went to stand, but Madigan shook her head, heading after Logan herself.

Chapter 16

Turning his head slightly, Logan peered through the night darkness as Madigan approached. He hadn't expected it to be her. He thought it would have been Silas.

"I love this time of night, Logan. Day's over and all the worries, stresses, cares, and burdens from the day can be laid at the Lord's feet. I don't need to carry them any more. I find comfort in that. It's something I have had to learn to do, to lay them down." She stood for a moment before she reached for a late summer rose. "I feel like a rose bud some days. I feel like marrying Silas the way we did robbed me of something, of being courted and wooed and planning a wedding. Then, I look at the man I love and realize that how and when we married doesn't matter. What matters is that we have one another." She stopped speaking, lost in memories for a moment. She then spoke, her voice low in the night. "There are people who said we rushed into it. Greg is the one who married us. We talked long and hard with him before we took the step." She peered at Logan through the night. "I have no idea where you and Aveleen are as a couple. I know she needs you in a way I have never seen before. Don't let that be the reason you marry."

"It's not." Logan sighed, his shoulders rising and falling. "I mean, it's part of it but not the whole reason. I love her more than I thought I could love anyone. I just want her safe." He blinked rapidly. "I just don't know if I can keep her safe."

"And you want to. Pray long and hard, Logan." She turned and walked away, meeting Silas in the doorway, looking around him for Aveleen. "Where's Aveleen?"

"She asked if there was a bedroom she could use. She's fading, Madi. She needs to sleep. Whatever it was she went through is still affecting her physically."

"Okay. I'll check on her." She looked over her shoulder. "I don't know if I got through to him, love."

"Leave him. They have a lot to think through, more I think than we did. Our danger was right in front of us."

"Theirs isn't, is it? It's much more subtle. Aveleen told me she recognized one of the men and that set off this chain of events." She walked into her husband's hug. "I hurt so much for them."

"I know you do. Go on. Check on Aveleen. I'll be here." He dropped a kiss on her cheek and watched her walk away from him.

Logan spoke from where he stood just outside the door. "How did you two ever do it?"

"God, Logan. That's the only way. Our church has supported us immensely."

Logan nodded. "Where's Aveleen? Bed already? She's exhausted. I want this over for her sake."

"We know you do. Listen, did you go through everything that Greg sent?"

Staring first at Silas and then the table, Logan finally shook his head. "No, I don't think I did. It can wait until morning. Do you have a couch I can crash on?"

"Better than that. An extra room, next door to Aveleen. Head on up."

Three hours later, Logan shot up from his bed, running for the door, his hand reaching for the knob to the bedroom door where Aveleen had sought her rest.   He shoved open the door, his eyes searching for her, finding her sitting up the edge of the bed, arms covering her head, as she sobbed, fear and terror coming through.   He approached carefully, sitting beside her before he reached to wrap arms around her. She fought him until she finally sank against him, knowing it was him that held her. Sobs continued, lessening in severity.   Logan looked up to see Madigan standing near them, Silas in the doorway.

He shook his head at the question on Madigan's face before he spoke in a low voice.   "This is what happens, Madigan. Silas. I'm so sorry. I didn't expect it to hit so hard."

Madigan dropped to a sitting position at the end of the bed, Silas standing behind her with a hand on her shoulder. "She's like this? Often?" At his nod, she shuddered. "Oh, Logan! What a way to live! Is she better with you near her?"

"She is." He looked down at Aveleen, his heart on his face, agony mixing with the love. "I just want to make her better and I can't."

Silas' voice broke through the silence that ensued, his prayer lifting Aveleen and Logan up to God. Logan could feel Aveleen calming and knew when she raised her head, a hand coming up to swipe at her face. Madigan rose and then returned, a warm cloth in her outstretched hand. Aveleen took it, looking up at the other couple, ready to apologize when her words froze on her lips.

Madigan turned to look at Silas, who stood, staring at Aveleen, a puzzled look on his face.

"Aveleen?" Logan's words caused her to jump and she turned to him.

"Logan, where are we?"

"We're with Silas and Madigan. Do you not remember?"

"I think so." She turned to look at Silas. "Do you have a brother?"

He shook his head. "No. I don't. Why?"

She continued to stare at him. "Because you look and sound like one of my abductors. And I know it's not you."

Silas stood, silent, trying to comprehend just what she was saying. "I do have some cousins I haven't seen in a long time. Tomorrow, I'll see if I can find pictures of them and show you."

She finally nodded, her head falling against Logan as she yawned, her eyes closing as she slept. He stood, tucking her back into her bed before he stooped to drop a kiss on the scar on her face and then turned away, following the other couple from the room.

"Thank you. I'm sorry she disturbed you."

"Not a problem, Logan. We'll see you in the morning."

Logan stood at the bedroom window, staring out at the moonlight yard, his heart lifting in prayer for his lady. He didn't see the red sparks from the cigarette held by the man at the end of the yard, who stood watching the house, his eyes finding Logan's window. They had been found.

Chapter 17

Three days later, Aveleen stood in the bridal shop, surrounded by gorgeous gowns, but her thoughts were not on them. She pictured her mother and grew sober. Madigan watched her face, knowing Aveleen wouldn't be buying a dress today. She drew her aside.

"Aveleen?"

"I can't, Madigan. I just can't." Tears hovered near the surface of her eyes. "I hate this. I have cried more in the last few months than I ever have in my whole life." She bit at her lip. "I need my family with me. I can't do this behind their backs."

"Then, that's what we'll do. Come, let's find you a dress. You can sent pictures to your Mom and she can help you decide that way. It's not the same, I know, but she can be part of it." She drew out her own phone and sent a text to Silas. "Silas can work on getting your family here."

"He can do that? But what will Logan say?" Aveleen was torn, her eyes on a particular dress.

"Logan will do what he feels is best for you. If it means waiting for your family, then he will."

"But his family!"

"Let the guys worry about that. We need to find you a dress." Madigan paused, her eyes on Aveleen's face. "Have you found one?"

Aveleen nodded. "I think I have. This one."

Silas looked up from his phone, searching for Logan in the backyard before he walked towards him. Logan looked up, a bleak look on his face, causing Silas to frown.

"Logan? Why the look?"

Logan handed over his phone. "This. I just got this email from Caleb. Whoever it is that's after us has found us. He didn't say how he knew. This puts you two at risk." Logan spun to stare at the end of the yard before walking that way. He was frustrated, beyond frustrated, he thought. How did they find us?

"Did they check your car before you left?" Silas' voice was quiet beside him

"No, they didn't. To tell you the truth, I was just thinking of getting Aveleen away." He pointed to the ground. "There. He stood there smoking." He looked around. "How do I tell her?"

"I think she already knows. Madi said she had a melt down at the bridal stop. Won't pick out a dress until you tell her you'll bring her family to her. And she's worried about your family." Silas watched Logan for a moment. "We'll work it out. I talked to Greg.   Abe has volunteered his plane and pilot to bring everyone here, your family as well, and then fly them back."

Logan shook his head, then paused. "It might work. But it would be putting you at risk."

"That we can work around.   I've talked to some friends on the force. They can call in volunteers to surround us and make sure nothing happens." Silas paused, a slight smile on his face. "That is, if you're wanting that. We do nothing without your input and that of Aveleen."

"Thank you. Let me talk to her." He paused as he felt his phone vibrate and pulled it out, a smile crossing his face. "She said she found what she wanted, and what time is she to be ready?" He looked up, catching the grin on Silas' face. "Is that my answer? Then go ahead, talk to who you need to."

Silas nodded, his eyes on the ground. "Whoever found you was out here. These cigarette butts weren't here yesterday." He stooped for a moment before he looked around. "I have no idea how to keep you two safe."

Logan paled as he saw the debris before he looked at Silas, determination on his face. "Do you have a computer I can use? I need to do some research." He held up a hand. "If you weren't told, I was a reporter, doing guest columns now. This seems too familiar to me." He spun in a circle. "The name she's remembering isn't correct. I think I might have it figured out."

"Sure. In my office." The two men headed for the house, Silas pointing out his computer to Logan before he headed for the kitchen.

Aveleen stood for a moment watching Logan's concentration before she walked towards him, his head rising as he felt her near him, a smile lighting up his face as he stood and reached for her.

"Did you find something?" At her nod, he tilted his head. "Does your Mom know?"

His gentle voice drew a longer hug from her. "She does. She loves it. Just wishes she could have been here."

"Abe's pilot is flying everyone in and out, Silas said. I told him to go ahead with that. We'll coordinate a date with them." He sat back down in the chair, drawing her down with him. "We've been found but Silas said precautions have been taken." He turned to look at the computer screen. "And I think I found your company."

"You did?"

"I did. It's close to what they asked you. And no I won't tell you. It's safer if you don't know."

"I need to know, Logan." She paused as he shook his head. "It's that bad?"

"I think it could be. I put out some feelers to some friends. They'll get back to me. It's not just an investment company. It's a front for drugs. How honest was your boss?"

"Honest, I think. But you're not sure."

"No, I'm not. Not any more. Not until I get the information I need."

She laid her head against his, her eyes on the computer screen, knowing he couldn't see her but realizing he would know she had peeked. "What are we to do, Logan? We can't continue to run, but we can't put others at risk by staying put."

His arms tightened around her. "That's a real worry, isn't it? I want so much to keep you safe and it's almost impossible to do just that." He pointed a finger towards the door. "We could walk away from this and from each other, right now, right at this point, but I don't want to. I want whatever time God gives us."

"Me, too." Her voice was barely a whisper. "Did I really wake everyone up the other night?"

"You did." He tilted his head to watch her face. "Are you remembering something?"

"I think I am. I need to search a name." She sighed, her face flushing as she spoke. "Did I really accuse Silas?"

"No, you didn't. You asked if he had a brother. He hasn't been able to find pictures of his cousins, but I have their names. I was about to search for them when you walked in."

"Then, do it. I need to know, Logan. I need to know if I have to apologize to him or not."

He searched the names, her hand pausing his when he brought up a picture. He felt the tremor in her hand and looked up at her, seeing the whiteness of her face.

"Is that one of them?"

She shook her head. "No, not that I remember. But I know him. I've seen him around and I didn't get a really good, safe feeling. He seemed to be watching me."

They both jumped as they heard Silas speak. "Which one, Aveleen?"

"Roger."

Silas sighed, then nodded, sadness covering his face. "I suspected him. He's always been a black sheep in the family, in trouble with his parents, the educational system, and law enforcement since he was really young. I haven't seen or heard from him in something like ten years or more. Nor have his parents." He hesitated. "You'll need to pass that name on to Caleb, Logan."

Logan watched with compassion as shoulders slumping, Silas walked away, heading to find his wife and let her know what had been discovered.

"Logan? How sure are you about his cousin?" Aveleen's voice was quiet.

"Fairly sure. Caleb's looking into it, seeing as it affects you, but he indicated he knew the name." Logan's eyes rested on the window across from where they were sitting. "We need to make more decisions, Aveleen."

"I know. Where to live. Where to go. What to do for work." She sighed. "I'm just not ready to do that but we have to."

"I know, Sweetest. One day at a time." He studied her face. "Where do we go from here?"

"Back to your town or back to mine? Holly's town? But wherever we go, I'll bring danger with me."

"I know. We need this over with and I don't see it happening any time soon." He reached for his phone he had set on the desk. "It's my Dad. Do you mind if I talk to him?" When she shook her head, he answered. "Dad? You're calling me? What's up? Oh. I see. Okay. You did? Tell me she didn't." Aveleen looked at him in surprise as he groaned. "Larkin is putting herself in danger, Dad. She needs to step back from that. I know. She won't listen to anyone, will she? What's that? The wedding? We're still working on that. Has someone been in touch with you? Who? Abe? Oh, Ian. I think that's his pilot. Aveleen's nodding so I guess that's correct. That's right. They're making the arrangements for us. We just have to confirm a date." He looked at the lady he was holding and smiled. "You'll love her, Dad. That much I know." He listened for a while before he blinked rapidly to clear his eyes. His voice barely above a whisper, he responded. "Thank you, Dad. Love you. Give Mom my love." He set his phone back down and tightened his hug on Aveleen.

"Logan? You're scaring me. What did your Dad say?"

He shook his head for a moment. "He wants to meet you, both he and Mom. He said welcome to the family. They love you already just because I do."

She nodded, knowing he was speaking what he had been told, but not sure that it was in fact the truth. She knew he was at risk just by being with her, but she just couldn't send him away. She needed him in her life and she suspected he needed her.

Chapter 18

Logan turned as he heard quiet footsteps behind him. His sister, Larkin, stood there, a puzzled look on her face. He was ready for angry words or a fight. That seems to be how she operated the last few years. He knew she was struggling, had been for a while, but he was at a loss as to how to help her.

"Larkin?"

She approached, reaching to hug him. "Logan? What's going on? You, too?"

"What do you mean, you too?"

"Danger. What is with you and Lincoln?" She sounded worried but disgruntled as well.

He gave a small grin. "When the ladies we love are in danger, that puts us there as well. I don't know if I can rightly explain it."

She shook her head even as she walked around the room. "I wish you could. I know I almost blew it with Holly and

Lincoln. I don't want to do that with you and Aveleen. I know we've had our differences lately, but you are my brother."

Logan watched as she paced, knowing there was more to what she wanted to ask, but also knew she wouldn't.

"Larkin, I can't explain it. There's too much danger out there right now. You're only here for a while. Get to know my lady, please?"

She stared at him before she shrugged and walked away. Logan watched her go, knowing that he would need to have the same conversation with her over and over. He had had to do that about Holly. He frowned. There was something going on with her and there had been for a while now, since before Lincoln had disappeared. She refused to say what but every once in a while, he saw real fear in her eyes when she didn't think someone was watching her.

He turned as he heard footsteps. Lincoln stood there, watching their sister before he looked at Logan.

"Everything okay?"

Logan shrugged. "I have no idea. Larkin isn't herself. She hasn't been in months, if not years."

"I know. Something happened on that last long trip she took and she has refused to talk about it. I've tried, Mom and Dad have tried. You two just don't communicate any more."

Logan sighed. "I know. I hate that. Now, what can I do for you?"

Lincoln gave a quick grin. "Nothing. Everything's ready for tomorrow?"

"It is." Logan gave a quick look around. "I have a bad feeling, Lincoln. I just don't like the way I getting a bad vibe about tomorrow."

"Then why wait until tomorrow? Have your wedding today."

Logan shook his head. "No, I won't do that to Aveleen. It's hard enough on her as it is."

Lincoln nodded. "I know it is. It was hard on Holly not having her parents there on her day. Even though her Dad was still alive at that point, she thought he had abandoned her and died somewhere."

Logan nodded. "I know. Listen, I have something to ask you." Before he could pose his question, their father appeared with a question of his own, leaving his two sons to shake their heads and promise to speak again. That promised talk never did happen.

The next afternoon, Logan stood, watching his bride as she talked with her brothers. Aubrey had welcomed him to the family. Avery had just given a curt nod and turned away. Logan sighed. Avery was so much like Larkin it was frightening. Both were going through something that no one knew about.

He felt a hand on his shoulder and looked to the side. His father stood there, Silas on his other side.

"I don't have to say anything, son. You know that taking this step is a huge leap of faith on both your parts."

"I know, Dad. I think we have just stirred the pot, as they say, and things are only going to get worse." Logan turned once more to watch Aveleen, seeing her eyes raised to him and a peaceful smile on her face. "We're leaving soon. And no, I won't tell you where we're heading. Not that it's that much of a secret. It's just that it's safest for you all."

"We know that. It's just very hard. We had this with Lincoln and now you. I just pray we don't have it with Larkin."

Logan nodded, then excused himself to go towards Aveleen, who walked towards him and into his embrace. He spoke for a moment and she nodded before she headed for the house. Silas and Madigan had opened their home up for the wedding and Logan knew it had been at risk for them.

Thirty minutes later, he frowned. Aveleen shouldn't have taken this long to be ready to leave. He searched for her, not finding her outside and then he headed inside. She was not to be found. Panic began to set in and he ran for the front door, pulling it open and sliding to a halt on the porch. He saw the dark van across the street and ran towards it. It pulled away from the curb as he approached it, hitting him and sending him flying through the air to land in a crumpled heap on the street. He didn't hear Aveleen's cry of despair as the van disappeared.

Shouts surrounded him as the men ran towards him, the police officers on duty heading for their vehicles. How this had happened, no one knew. All they knew was that Logan was down and Aveleen had disappeared, once more.

Logan felt the hands on him, turning him over, assessing him before he was loaded onto a stretcher and sent on his way to the hospital, his father in the vehicle with him. He groaned as he roused more fully, his eyes searching for Aveleen.

"Aveleen?" When his father didn't respond, Logan's eyes slid closed. "She's gone again, isn't she, Dad?"

"They're looking for her, son. They have a good description of the van. Rest. We're at the hospital." His father stepped out and waited as the stretcher was off-loaded and wheeled into the Emergency department.

Liam turned to find Leigh, Lincoln and Holly, and others he didn't recognize standing there.

An hour later, Caleb walked in towards him, a frown on his face. "How's Logan?"

"I'm sorry. I don't think I know you." Liam stood, a puzzled look on his face.

Caleb shook his head. "Sorry. I'm Chief Caleb Logan from Riverville. I was here in town helping provide security for Aveleen and Logan." He nodded towards the examination rooms. "How is he?"

Liam shook his head. "I haven't heard yet. I'm trying to get that information." He looked around. "Any word on Aveleen?"

Caleb didn't respond and Liam's heart sank. How could he tell his son his bride was still missing? "No word?"

"No. Whoever took her made their escape. It's starting all over for her."

"Logan won't let it rest. He'll be up and out of here looking for her in short order."

"That's true, Dad." Logan spoke from behind him. "Caleb? No word? Then we'll head back to Riverville. That's where they'll take her." He grimaced as he moved towards the door, not seeing his mother coming towards him.

Liam reached for his wife, his arm around her and then the other catching his daughter close. "Let him go, Leigh. He needs to be doing something. We'll catch up with him." He looked to the ceiling, his heart raising in prayer for his son and new daughter-in-law.

Logan stared out the window of Caleb's cruiser as Caleb made the turn back into the downtown area of Riverville. "Where would they take her, Caleb?"

"That I don't know. We never did find the original house she was in here. And they did have her in Cairn to begin with."

"Talk to Dougal on an official basis, please. I know Holly would have already called him."

"I have already. He's on the lookout but he doesn't seem to think they'll bring her back there. I have to agree with him. I don't think they will either. I would suspect somewhere around Riverville or Hope."

Logan nodded, his eyes sliding closed in prayer. "Why now, Caleb? Why wait until we were married?"

"To use you against her. It is one thing to use a boyfriend but a husband is stronger leverage."

Logan walked slowly up the sidewalk to his house, noting the crime scene tape still moving in the breeze. He had momentarily forgotten the break in. What had they been after? He didn't hear Caleb's footsteps behind him until Caleb spoke.

"Let me go in with you, Logan."

Logan shook his head. "No. Go home, Caleb. You need to be with your family. Thank you." He shut the door and locked it, leaning back against it, his hands holding the side of his head, a headache making its presence known. He had been lucky, the doctors said. No broken bones. Just bruising but that would hurt, they told him. His heart hurt worse, aching for his lady, and praying that she was alive and unharmed.

He walked the house, finally stopping in his office, seeing the scattered files and tumbled books. He stepped over the piles and sank into his desk chair, a sigh drawn from deep within him. His head sank to his outstretched arms as he prayed and then slept.

Dawn found him rising, startled awake by something. He prowled the house and then slipped outside to walk the house and then the yard. Nothing stood out at him. So what had awakened him?

He turned back to the house, finally seeing the note tacked to the shutter at the bedroom window. He sighed. So this is it, is it, Lord? Protect my Sweetest, please?

He reached for the envelope, finding Aveleen cross necklace inside, but no letter. A warning, he supposed, that he was not to talk to anyone. He was conflicted, knowing he had to talk to Caleb and not wanting to do anything to put his lady at more risk.

Chapter 19

He stood for a moment staring around his office, a frown on his face. Logan felt something off in the room but didn't know what. He turned to the piles on the floor before he looked at his desk, moving that way, sinking into the leather chair he had purchased to replace his old one. Aveleen had pushed him to do just that.

He stared at the desk before an arm came out and swept the top clean, shoving the papers and books and notes flying to the floor. He reached for the plain white mug that held his pens, pencils and highlighters, studying it for a moment before his arm went back and he pitched the mug across the room, to shatter against a wall, the clatter of the pens and pencils hitting the floor sounding loud. His head dropped to the cleared desk as he sobbed. He didn't hear the doorbell or the opening of the front door, or the sounds of footsteps and a voice calling for him.

He finally looked up to see Dave sitting across from him, contemplating the floor.

"Dave? I'm sorry. I didn't hear you."

"Not a problem, Logan. I didn't think you did. I just wanted to see how you were doing." He looked around before a grin lit his face. "I can see just how that is."

Logan groaned as he looked around, seeing the mess he had created. "I was angry." He sighed as he rose, bending to start picking up the papers.

Dave moved to help him. "Where do you want these?"

Logan nodded towards the low table at the end of the room. "On there for now, I guess. I have to sort through them. Whoever searched my house trashed this room at the time."

"I can see that." Dave paused, his hand on Logan's arm stilling his movements. "Listen. Don't worry about the anger, fear, lack of trust, questions you have. God understands each one. I went through the whole gamut with Rylee."

Logan studied his friend for a moment. "Thank you. You know how I feel."

"To some extent I do. Don't let anyone tell you they know exactly how you feel. They can't. The only one who can is God. Even when you can't articulate a word, He knows."

Logan nodded, before looking down at the papers he held, not seeing them for a moment before his vision sharpened. "Dave. This isn't mine." He held up a photo. "I have no idea who this is."

Dave leaned over to study it. "That's the lawyer Aveleen was working for. That's his brother. Why would that photo be here?"

Logan's face tightened. "I have no idea. Aveleen didn't leave it. I didn't have it." He looked at Dave. "Whoever trashed the place dropped it. Now, was that on purpose or an accident?"

Dave's phone was out. "We need Frankie here." He stopped as Logan's hand came out as he shook his head. "Logan? We need to report this."

"Not at the moment. Let me think about it while we finish cleaning. I want to go through every room of the house. With you here as a witness, maybe I'll begin to find some answers."

Two hours later, Logan stood once more in his office, his eyes on the photo as he listened to Dave and Frankie talk in the front room. He had finally agreed to bring Frankie in, but he wished he hadn't. Frankie would want to take the photo. He shot a look over his shoulder and moved away, to his printer, to make a copy. He hid the original, not wanting to give it up.

Frankie stood for a moment, contemplating the room and then Logan. "Logan? Did you find anything other than that photo?"

"No. I didn't think I would. I haven't looked outside but I doubt I'll find anything there. Any word?" He sighed as Frankie shook his head. "I didn't think there would be. It's a waiting game now."

"That it is. Where is the photo?"

Logan handed it over. "I've never met those men. Dave says one of them was Aveleen's employer."

"He was. There have been rumours about him and about his brother for years. Nothing we could pin down." He stared at the photo, a frown on his face. "This wasn't taken around here. That much I know."

"Where would it have been taken then?" Logan leaned over to look closer, a frown on his face. "That's in Hope. That's a park near the downtown. What is going on?"

"Were you investigating them?"

Logan shook his head. "No. I didn't do crime or courts reporting. I was out there with traffic sometimes, with education, with happy events as we called them." Then he shook his head. "I found an envelope outside on a shutter. It had her locket in it."

"Where's the envelope?" He took it from Logan. "Nothing on it. I doubt we'll find any fingerprints other than yours."

"I doubt that. There was no note. Just the locket." He pulled it from his pocket, fingering it before he returned it. "No. I'm not letting you have it."

Frankie paused, then shrugged. "Sure. I doubt we'd find anything on it." He looked around. "Dave had to run. He's going on duty. What can I do for you?"

"Find my bride. And that's not going to be easy, that much I know." Logan blinked rapidly to clear his vision. "Thanks, Frankie." He turned and walked away, the back door closing behind him.

Frankie hesitated a moment before he left, not quite happy with how the conversation had gone. Logan was up to something, that much he knew. He would be too, if it was him.

Logan paced his backyard, his thoughts on the photo. There was something about it that concerned him. Why was it taken in Hope? What was the connection to him? Was it left on purpose or by accident?

He spun and stared at the house, then ran for his car, his keys in his hands. He hadn't been to Aveleen's yet and needed to go there. Who knew what he would find there.

He searched outside her house and then entered, feeling the staleness of the air from the house being closed up for days. He searched the house, seeing the same state as his had been in. He spent hours straightening the rooms, not finding anything that would help find her. He paused, shaking his head. That idea hadn't worked, he thought.

He stood on the front walk, staring at the gardens. No, nothing was off there. Now, what, he wondered? How did he find his lady?

He sat in his car, staring ahead, before he sighed and pulled away, not seeing the van following him. He drove away from Riverville, heading where he had no idea. Ending up in Hope, he paused at a local coffee shop before going in, nodding at the clerk before he turned and left without making a purchase. This was stupid, he thought. She's not here, so why am I?

Daylight found him prowling the park in the picture, not finding anything that would help. He stood for a moment, hand on his head, before he headed for his parents. Then he stopped. No, he couldn't go there. That would put them in danger.

He headed his car out of town again, this time back towards Riverville. Why, he had no idea. He just knew that's where he had to be. Aveleen was near there, he thought. He could feel her presence better there than anywhere else.

A week had passed by the time the second letter was left, this time with a picture from their wedding. He sighed, his heart hurting for his lady. They had been that close to them all the time. How could that have been? When he asked Frankie, he studied the photo and said a telephoto lens more than likely. He wanted to take the picture for evidence. Logan finally gave it to him, reluctance in his gesture. He wanted his lady home but that wasn't to be. Lord, he prayed, keep her safe and well. Bring her back to me, please.

Chapter 20

Three weeks after their wedding, Logan had taken to wandering the streets at any hour of the day or night, searching for what he didn't know. When he was at home, he was deep into research, trying to find the men responsible. Emma was helping, using the resources of her own investigative business to help. Whoever the men were, they had hidden themselves well. Little bits and pieces were coming together but not enough to point a finger at the leader or even the men involved. There had been no more communication from the abductors. That concerned Logan. He had talked long with Aubrey about who Aveleen had been in contact with over the years, but he could shed little light on her contacts. He indicated that in the last eighteen months or so, she had spoken little about her work, other than saying she was ready to move on, to find something else to do. Why, Aubrey didn't know. Logan could get little information from Avery, who blamed him for his sister's disappearance. Aubrey had shrugged, his face dark with anger towards his brother.

Logan stood for a moment, eying his computer before he sank down into the chair. He pulled his keyboard towards him and began to rapidly type. He had a column due that day and needed to work on it. Lost in thought, he ignored his phone ringing, reaching to mute it, and ignored the doorbell and the pounding at his door. He finally sent the column away to his editor and sat back, drained. He frowned. He reached for his phone, seeing that Caleb had been trying to reach him. He rose, heading for the door, pulling it open, finding Frankie standing there, hand raised to pound at the wood again.

"Frankie?"

"Where have you been, Logan? We've been trying to reach you."

"Working. I guess I just got lost in the column and ignored everything around me." He looked around, seeing Dave waiting by Frankie's car. "What is going on?"

"We need you to come with us. We may have found a house where Aveleen was."

Logan stared at him, hope rising within him. "You've found her?"

"No. Not yet. But it looks as if they left in a hurry." Frankie shoved Logan towards his car. "In. We need to get out there."

Logan watched as Frankie walked towards the tape strung around the house. It was out in the country, hidden from sight by the trees. He turned to ask Dave something, but found Dave engrossed in watching the activity, a strained look on his face. Logan sighed. This must be bringing back bad memories for both men, he thought. He shoved open his door and then stood, leaning against the car, his eyes tracing the trees around before he walked away from the car, heading into the woods. He heard Dave call him and then heard his footsteps behind him.

"Logan?"

"Dave, look. This trail is well worn. It shouldn't be. So why is?" Logan went to move forward, to find his arm locked in Dave's hand and himself pulled backwards.

"We're not going there. We're going back to talk with Frankie. This is likely part of the crime scene. We can't contaminate it."

Logan reluctantly moved back, watching as Frankie headed their way, spoke briefly with Dave and then walked towards the path Logan had found. He was gone for close to an hour before he returned, deep in conversation with a crime scene tech. Frankie looked up to find Logan's gaze fixed on him before he nodded and then walked towards him.

"Frankie?"

"We found evidence Aveleen was taken out that way. The path was protected from the rain to some degree. We can't determine what kind of vehicle was waiting. That's been washed away by the rain."

Logan was frustrated. "How long?"

Frankie shrugged. "We have no idea, Logan. That's what the techs will try and determine. Come on. We need to leave." He watched with compassion as Logan turned back to the house. "I can't let you go in there. You know that."

Logan nodded. "I know. Just tell me, Frankie. Is she still alive?"

"She is. That much I can tell you. How she is, that I can't. None of us can."

Logan gave a grim nod. "I know you can't. As long as she's alive, there's hope." He slid into the car, laying his head back and closing his eyes, his heart and mind consumed with prayer for his lady.

He paced his house for a while after Frankie left, his thoughts muddled before he reached for a pad of paper and a pen, sliding them onto the kitchen table as he made himself a sandwich and a cup of tea. Sitting, he pushed the food away and pulled the paper to him, listing all the questions, comments and whatever else came to his mind. He stared at it for a while before he rose and rapidly walked back to his office, finding the rolls of newsprint and taping them to his walls, taking one page to write each question, comment, thought. He turned finally, surprised at the number of pages up. He didn't care. He would work through each one, until he solved this and found his lady.

Caleb stared at his work later that night, then shook his head. "Are you sure you won't come work for me? This is what we do."

"No, Caleb. No, I'm not cut out for that. This is what I do. Not on this scale, by any means. But I research for my articles. Every article has a folder that has proof in it for what I write." He turned in a circle. "I just wish this would bring her home quickly."

Caleb had been reading some of the thoughts and comments. "You've done a lot of work. Some of this we haven't even got to. Why?"

Logan shrugged. "I have no idea. It's just how my mind works. It always has done this." He looked around. "I didn't realize I was putting up so many until I was done. There are a lot of unanswered questions, aren't there?"

"That there are." Caleb looked at Logan, trying to assess him. "How are you really doing, Logan?"

He shrugged. "I have no idea how I'm supposed to be doing. How would you be?" He sighed. "I apologize. It's not your fault. I shouldn't have bit."

"It's okay. That's what friends are for." Caleb glanced at his watch. "I have to run. Hannah asked if you would come for supper."

Logan shook his head. "Thank Hannah for me, but not tonight."

Chapter 21

Another month had passed. Logan had grown thin and stress showed on his face. His family and friends tried to help him but he shoved them away. Aveleen's family was there, helping where he would let them, but even that he put a stop to. He felt he was a danger to anyone who came near him and he refused to put anyone else in danger. There had been no further word from her abductors. He was beginning to give up hope that he would see her again.

A knock at his door one day surprised him, bringing him back from the research he was deep into. He stared at Avery, who stood there, hesitation in his demeanour.

"Logan? Can we talk?"

Logan shrugged, before he stepped back, letting Avery enter. "The kitchen, I think. What can I get you?"

"Tea or water, whichever is easiest." Avery sank into a chair, his hands rubbing nervously together.

Setting a mug of tea in front of the younger man, Logan sat across from him, waiting for Avery to speak.

"Logan, I need to apologize to you. I haven't treated you very well and I'm sorry. Aveleen told me off before she disappeared. She stated you had nothing to do with her abduction and that I needed to give you a chance." He looked up. "Was she right?"

"About me being involved in her abduction?" Logan shrugged. "I have no idea. I'm finding evidence that I might have been on the edge of what was going on, just from being a reporter, but I don't have concrete proof. Why do you ask?"

Avery shrugged. "I've heard rumours around town, that Aveleen was taken in the first place because of someone she knew, not from what she did. I just wondered if you had come across any evidence of that."

Logan sighed. "Not really. There's something there I just haven't found yet. Some name that I need and don't have." He pointed to his walls. "That's what I've been up to." He shot a look at Avery. "What is it you do for work anyway?"

"I run the homeless shelter for men. Why?"

"That's what I'm missing." Logan was on his feet, his eyes searching his paper. "Here. I had a tentative name and rumour, about someone who was homeless and I haven't been able to track him down."

Avery stared at the walls. "You've done all this?" He walked through the rooms, reading the papers. "Has Caleb asked you to join the force?"

Logan laughed. "He has and I said no. I don't want that. I'm not sure where I'm heading once Aveleen's back, but we'll make that decision together."

"I pray that she's back soon." Avery turned. "What's with your sister?"

"What do you mean?" Logan turned to watch him. "What are you picking up?"

"She's running from something or someone. She has that look I see on the men in the shelter sometimes. Back to the shelter. What name were you looking for? I can't confirm it, confidentiality and all that, but if he's still there, I'll talk to him and see if I can get him to speak with you."

"That would be great. Here." Logan quickly scrawled the name of a scrap of paper and handed it over. "There's something else, isn't there?"

Avery looked at the paper before he looked up. "There is. Aubrey mentioned that you were the only one who could calm Aveleen. How did you do that?"

Logan shrugged. "God, I guess. He used me to calm her. I just worry about how she's doing now, away from us. God has to be the One to calm her now."

Avery nodded. "Listen. I plan to hike out behind that house they said she was held in on Saturday. I'd welcome you to come with me."

"What time and where do we meet?" Logan didn't hesitate. "I've been wanting to explore that area and just haven't made it out there yet."

"Plan on spending Saturday night then. There's a cabin we can use." Avery hesitated before he extended his hand. "Thank you for understanding, Logan."

Logan shrugged. "We have to work together to find her."

Early that Saturday morning, Logan locked his car and turned to Avery. "Lead the way. You know where you're planning on going. I don't."

Avery pointed towards a path. "Let's go that way. It leads behind the house and then through the woods. I can't say for sure that's where they went but I want to walk it. It leads to the cabin I told you about."

"Would not Caleb's team have checked it out?"

"I'm sure they did, but I know how Aveleen thinks. Or how she did. Her thought processes seemed to have changed."

"I am sure they did. Others have commented on it. She told me she didn't think the same way as she did before." He paused before he continued, repeated himself. "That's what I understand. I can't explain that, Avery. I am not sure she even can. What she went through changed her. She'll never be the same sister you had."

"I know. That grieves me, Logan. I want that sister back." He paused, his eyes seeking the sky. "We have a ways to go today. Let's get moving."

"What exactly are we looking for?"

Avery shrugged. "I have no idea. I guess we'll know when we see it."

Logan pushed through the woods and into the long grass, his eyes on the path, a frown in place. How was he to know, after all these weeks, if Aveleen had been along here? How would Avery even know himself?

Avery finally stopped, turning to Logan. "I think we're about half way there. This is where they would likely have rested, if at all. I can't see them pushing through without a stop. They're not used to this, not likely."

"No, I wouldn't suspect that they are. If they're city folks, they won't have gone this far, would they?" Logan dropped his pack and looked around. "There. That looks like a resting spot."

Avery nodded. "I think it is. Logan, what are we looking for again?"

"Any sign of them or Aveleen. And I don't see anything. Not now. I would say it's likely been too long." Logan paused, feeling watched. "Someone's here, Avery. I can feel the eyes."

"What are you talking about?" Avery paced in a circle. "There's no one here."

"No, there is. You won't see them. They'll stay hidden." Logan watched as Avery began to walk away from him. He turned suddenly, hearing a slight sound and seeing sunlight reflecting off metal. "Avery! Down!"

He launched himself towards Avery, his body taking the younger man to the ground, a heavy blow on his own back taking away his breath and then his vision blurred and he didn't hear Avery's complaints to get off him.

Avery's breath came in gasps as he shoved at Logan, twisting to do so. "Logan, get off me." He finally managed to get out from under Logan's weight, spinning to rise to his knees. "Just what is going on? What'd you do that for?" When Logan didn't respond, he reached to shake him, finding no response. "Logan? Come on. Stop fooling around. This is serious. Logan?" His hand found the wet spot on Logan's back and drew his hand towards him, shocked and sickened at the red stain that dripped to the ground. "Logan! Please! Tell me this isn't what I think it is!"

Logan lay silent, his breath shallow, as Avery tore at his flannel shirt and then his T-shirt, exposing the wound. Avery dumped his pack, reaching for the first aid kit, and frantically pulling out gauze pads, shoving them as hard as he could against the wound, hoping to stem the flow of blood. He reached for his phone, praying he had service.

An hour later he watched as the paramedics worked over Logan, starting the IV lines, the oxygen, the heart monitor. He prayed for his sister's husband, knowing this would not have happened if he hadn't persuaded him to come with him.

Frankie walked towards him, his eyes on Logan first, before he spoke. "Avery? Talk to me. What happened? Why were you two out here?"

"I talked Logan into coming with me. Grasping at straws, I guess. I thought maybe I could find something that would tell me Aveleen had been here." He was frantic, knowing Logan was clinging to life, from what he had overheard. "I didn't think anyone would be here. Neither did Logan."

"No, there shouldn't have been. But I think someone's been following him closely and knew what you two were planning. There is likely someone following you as well." Frankie sighed. "We searched and found nothing."

"I thought that." He looked towards the helicopter lifting from the area. "And now Logan might not make it. All because of me."

"No, not because of you, Avery. Talk to me. Tell me what happened." Frankie pointed back towards the trail. "That way. I want you under cover as soon as we can get you there."

"We were talking. Logan said this was a rest area. Then I moved away. Next thing I know he's taking me down. No warning." Avery looked around. "What happened?"

"I suspect Logan heard or saw something and moved to protect you. That's his character."

Avery shuddered. "After the way I treated him, he saved me."

"I gather you two have worked out your differences."

"We had. That's why we were out here today. Logan wanted to search this area too, only hadn't taken the time."

Frankie pointed to his car. "That's Logan's car?"

"It is. He drove this morning." Avery watched as Frankie sped back into town, heading for the hospital. "We need to call his family."

"Already done." Frankie parked, then placed a hand on Avery's arm. "Don't blame yourself, Avery. It's not your fault. Before we go in, let's pray."

Avery nodded. Once in the hospital, he dropped to a chair, his head down, fighting his emotions. Don't let him die, Lord. Please! Bring Aveleen home and soon.

Chapter 22

Liam and Leigh stood beside their son's bedside a day later. Liam studied the lines running to his son's body, listening to the beep of the monitors, the whizz and hiss of the ventilator and prayed, prayed harder than he had before in his life. The surgeon had talked to them. It didn't look good, he said. The bullet had been too close to the spine for them to be sure what damage had been done, not until Logan awoke. There were no guarantees that would happen either. The chances of him being crippled were strong, they were warned.

He looked around as he heard the door and saw Greg there. He had come to appreciate Aveleen's pastor over the last few hours.

Greg paused at the foot of the bed, his eyes on Logan, before he moved closer to the older couple.

"Any change?"

Leigh shook her head. "No. He's not rousing. Not at all." She wiped at her face with the damp cloth she held.

Greg nodded, his heart breaking for the couple. He knew Lincoln and Holly were in the chapel with Larkin, their weeks' old daughter with Greg's wife, Mary. He had left a group from the church there, Abe and Emma leading them.

"Let me pray with you. It may be all we have left to do, but God is in this situation. You both know that."

"We do. The surgeon says it will likely be a while before they take him off the ventilator. The bullet did some damage to a lung." Liam's hand rested on his son's shoulder. "Why, Greg?"

"Why? Why did it happen? Why did God allow it?" At Liam's nod, Greg shook his head. "I don't have those answers, Liam. I know Logan threw himself at Avery, taking the bullet meant for him." At Liam's look, he paused. "You didn't know that?"

Liam shook his head. "I thought it was meant for Logan. And it was meant for Avery?"

"It was. Avery is beside himself with guilt. These two had talked through their differences from what Avery has said. They were out there looking for Aveleen."

"I wondered why they were out there. I hadn't heard." Liam looked towards the door. "I need to talk to him."

"And you can. Right now, stay with Logan for as long as they'll let you. The nurse said another fifteen minutes or so and then they'd be in to ask you to leave for a while."

Three weeks later, Leigh stood at the window in the private room Logan had been moved to. He had been weaned off the ventilator and now breathed room air as they stated it. He was still hooked up to machines and that concerned her. She had almost given up that he would awaken once more. She heard a whisper of sound and spun, thinking she was the only one in the room. She stared, astounded, as she saw the slight form, the head of black curls, the arms that cradled Logan, heard the anguished sobs and low voice calling for Logan to awake. Aveleen? But how?

She moved towards Aveleen, finding Abe in her way, his hand on her arm drawing her from the room.

"Abe?"

He just shook his head. "Not now, Leigh. We'll explain. Right now, I need you to come with me. I'm putting my men on Logan's room. I want you and your family to be safe and that means we move you away from here." He shook his head as she protested. "We need to. They'll go after one of you if we don't."

Leigh looked towards her son and Aveleen, realizing that Aveleen didn't know she was there. She shook her head at Abe.

"No. Let me speak with Aveleen."

Abe's hand tightened on her arm. "You can't. Not yet. Frankie wants to speak with her first. He needs to. You understand she has to give a statement. They allowed her here to see Logan, but only for a bit."

Leigh nodded, her glance going to the young couple before the door closed behind her. "How, Abe?"

He shook his head again. "I can't go into the particulars. Not yet. It's not safe for anyone."

Aveleen heard the door close but her attention was on Logan. Abe had warned her he wasn't doing well, had explained what had happened, and that he had never awakened yet. She touched his face and then laid her head against his shoulder, silent sobs shaking her body. This was too much, she thought. She had asked where Logan was and was shocked when Abe had explained. She had been so thankful when his men had appeared just hours before, taking her away from her captors. She didn't know the details of how that happened, didn't know if she wanted to. She was just glad to be free.

She looked up as she heard footsteps approaching her. The surgeon stood there, watching her for a moment.

"Aveleen? Welcome home. I'll find someone to come check you out and get you some clean clothes." He nodded towards Logan. "Let me see how he is and then we'll talk."

She stepped back, taking the clothing the nurse had handed her and heading into the washroom to clean up. She listened through the closed door as she did so, hearing faint discussion but not able to make out the words. She stared at her pale, discoloured face. The bruising was in various colours. This time, the man hadn't cared that she was hurt. She frowned, not sure as to why that was.

She stopped near the bed, waiting for the surgeon to look up, turning at a touch on her arm, seeing John, a physician from the church, standing beside her.

"Aveleen, let me take a look at you. Abe called me to come and see you."

She sighed. "Now?"

"Yes, now. It's important that we get a picture of how you are right now." He drew her away from the bed and began his assessment, his hands gentle as he touched her bruising, his questions keen. "We'll do some blood work on you, but overall, I'd saw physically you're in good shape. Do you need to talk to anyone?"

She paused, her eyes on his face before she looked over at Logan. "Just

Logan." Her voice was so quiet, John wasn't sure he had heard her.

"That we can help with. But you need to understand what's going on with him." The surgeon stood beside John, and as he spoke, detailing Logan's condition and what he had been through, her eyes shifted from Logan to the surgeon and back again.

She didn't answer his questions, just rose and walked to the bed once more, her hand on Logan's arm, her other hand on his face. "Thank you. Please? Can I be alone with him?"

John's arm came around her in a hug. "That you can, Aveleen. Someone will be in and out to check on you. Frankie's coming in to see you in about fifteen minutes. He stated that was not an option. He wants your statement before you talk to anyone else."

She nodded, her head turning as she watched the men walk away, before she pulled a chair over to the bed, dropping into it, fatigue draining her strength. Why, Lord? Why Logan? What is the purpose in this?

Frankie stopped in the doorway, his eyes on his friend as she sat, her head down on the bed, her shoulders shaking. He frowned, knowing he had to disturb her and not wanting to.

Aveleen looked around as she heard Frankie approaching and sighed. "You want to talk to me, don't you?"

"I do, Aveleen. I need your statement. This time, it's not Caleb who's taking it. He's stepped back from the investigation. He won't even let me talk to him."

She nodded, swiping at a tear that had escaped. "I hate who I've become, Frankie. They've stolen so much from me. And from Logan. I was told he might not walk again. Who does this?"

"That is part of our investigation. Avery's been helping us, but he doesn't have a lot of information as to why. They were out there looking for you when it happened."

She sighed. "That's what Murphy O'Brien said when he walked me in here. Couldn't they leave the investigation to you?"

Frankie gave a quick grin. "Those two guys love you too much to do that. We warned them to not go out on their own but aside from arresting them, there wasn't much we could do." He pulled over a chair, brought out his small dictator, set it ready and looked over at her. "Let's get this over with. I'll tape it, have it transcribed, and then bring it back for you."

"What? No computer?"

Frankie laughed. "Not me. I'm old school, to some extent." He sobered, his eyes assessing her and her frame of mind. "We need to do this now, Aveleen. If you need to stop at any time, say so. It can become part of the statement that you needed a break."

She shook her head. "No. One shot is all you'll get."

Chapter 23

Sighing inwardly, Aveleen turned to look at Logan, finding he hadn't moved, her hand reaching to clasp his. Where did she start? Way back at the beginning, or when she had been abducted from Silas' home? Lord, I can't do this. I can't walk back through what I went through this time. Thank you that Logan won't hear it. I don't want him to. He'll be up out of that bed and hunting for the men if he does.

She looked at Frankie and nodded, watching as he reached for the dictator and started it, stating who was there, the date, time and the reason for the statement, before he nodded in turn at her.

Aveleen's other hand clenched on her leg. Lord, I need you. I can't do this. She finally looked up at Frankie, who was frowning at her before he gave her an encouraging smile and nod.

"I need to go back a few weeks before our wedding. Logan doesn't know that I kept receiving threats directed at him and at my family. The letters and pictures are in my safe. I will let you have the combination and you can retrieve them. They were becoming more vicious all the time.

"Anyway, back to when we left Riverville, Logan didn't tell me where we were heading. I was surprised to find it was only a short distance from here. I didn't know what he had planned, although I did have suspicions. We talked a lot while we were there, finally agreeing not to let fear drive our lives any more. Silas arranged for our families to come in and we had the wedding at his place. I didn't like that. I had a bad feeling about that."

She sighed, her thoughts going back to that day. "Everything was beautiful and almost perfect. Logan asked me to change into something casual as we were planning on heading out to a cabin he had rented. He didn't tell me where, just that I would like it.

"I headed up to change, packed my bag and then came back downstairs. I dropped the bag at the front door and stepped out on the porch for a moment. I didn't see the man standing near the steps until he reached for me, covering my mouth

217

before I could scream. I struggled with him, and I think I scratched his face. He carried me to the van and shoved me inside. At that point, I heard Logan and saw him running for me. I screamed at him and then someone held a cloth over my mouth. I struggled to get away but lost consciousness quickly."

She paused, taking the bottle of water handed to her and sipping. Her thoughts slipped back to the previous weeks and what she had been through.

She had awakened in the van, shoving herself upright and staring around, seeing one of the men standing near the open door. She could hear conversation but could not make out any of the words. Her head resting against the window, her thoughts drifted back to Logan. Let him be okay was her plea. She reached for the van door but it was locked and she couldn't open it. She wasn't even sure afterwards if she could have walked, let alone run, to get away. The men jumped back into the van and drove off, Aveleen's head bouncing against the window as she drifted off again.

When she roused again, she found herself being roughly pulled from the van and then shoved towards a building.   A factory, she thought, abandoned. She wasn't sure where she was at that point. She didn't recognize the building in the dark.   She realized that hours had passed since she had been taken again.   Lord, please be with Logan! Let him be alive!

She stumbled as she was pushed into a room, before she swayed on her feet, the chloroform or whatever she had been given still affecting her. She turned slowly, careful to keep her balance, and studied the room. Block walls with no windows.   A block ceiling and cement floor. Not a chance for her to escape this time, not from this room.

She finally sank to the floor in the centre of the room, her head on her folded arms and slept, her last thought a prayer for Logan. She didn't hear the door open or her abductor standing there, staring at her, gloating at having her back in his clutches. He stood for a moment before he turned and walked away.   This time, she would not escape, he vowed. She would give him the information she had and that he wanted. He knew she had it. It was just a matter of time before she turned it over to him.

Aveleen roused slowly the next day, shivering in the dampness and cold of the concrete block room. She sat up, her eyes on the door, her thoughts with Logan, praying for his safety. This time, she just knew in her heart she wouldn't get away. And she had no idea what the man wanted. She didn't know anything.

She didn't look up as the door opened and black suit-clad legs stopped in her line of vision. He spoke, but she didn't understand what he asked. A slap across the face sent her to the floor and her hand was raised to cup the hurt. She shook her head, not understanding still what he was asking.

Day by day, the same scenario played out. By the time a week or two had gone by, she understood what he wanted. He wanted names and account numbers. She tried to explain, in tears at times, that she didn't have that information.

She was moved after about ten days, a blindfold across her eyes to prevent her knowing just where she was. Another concrete room in another abandoned building, she thought. Despair and discouragement had begun to dog her. She grew silent, even with the abuse she suffered. She retreated within herself, not realizing this was how she had reacted before.

He brought in a computer and showed her that he had managed to find her program and made her log in. Her fingers hurt from the tight grip he had had on them when she refused. She tried to avoid that, but he had a grip on her hands that wouldn't let her go. She studied him when he had turned away and reached for the keyboard, typing quickly and sending a message to Caleb and then setting the program to delete itself.

His anger turned to rage when he walked back to her and saw the blank screen. The blows she suffered sent her to the floor, her hands not able to protect herself. He stood over her crumpled form, rage on his face, spittle flying from his mouth he was that angry. She lay still, not moving, not really aware of what was happening.

She was pulled to her feet, how much later she didn't know and didn't care about. She was shoved into the van once more, darkness hiding her from onlookers. She was taken to an abandoned mine, shoved into one of the shafts. She heard the nails being hammered home into boards across the entrance and knew she would not walk away from that room. She slid to the ground, unable to weep, the tears dried up within her. She couldn't pray, didn't think God heard or cared about her any more. She composed a love letter in her mind to Logan, but had no way of writing it down. She had no idea how long she had been gone by that point. She searched the room, moving slowly, the beating having taken more from her than she felt she had to give. She felt for anything that would write or that she could use for that. Finding a spike, she turned, desperate to leave some kind of letter to whoever would find her, naming who had taken her, what he had wanted and who was with him.

She paused, something deep within her rising to the surface of her mind. She shook her head, regretting it at the pain that went through it. No, she thought, he's not the leader. He's not the mastermind. He doesn't have it in him to be that. Doesn't have the smarts, as Dad would say. There has to be someone over him. But who? Her closed hand tapped at her forehead as she tried hard to think who it was. Horror spread through her as a name came up. No, she thought. Not that person. But she added the name to her list, the spike finally falling from her hand as she sank down, exhausted. She just knew this was it. She would never see Logan or her family again.

She didn't hear the furtive footsteps that made their way towards her or hear her name called in a low voice. She didn't rouse when the boards were pulled away from the entrance or see the filtered light was shone around the room, its beam finding her. She didn't hear her name called again as the man in the dark clothing dropped to his knees beside her, feeling for a sign of life, and then looking up to nod before he gathered her into his arms and headed back the way she had been brought so many hours or days before. When asked, she could give no time for how long she had been there. All she could remember was that it had felt like forever.

She didn't hear the quiet conversation behind her as other men searched the room, finding the board she had scratched her thoughts on, bringing it out with them. She didn't feel the gentle hands laying her on a bed in a camper or feel the hands that moved over her, seeking to find any broken bones. She flinched as bruises were touched. She roused as she heard voices talking around her and felt her hand being gently bound on a splint.

She looked around her, terror on her face, her mouth open to scream when a familiar voice spoke to her. She stared at him in fear until she recognized him.

"Abe?" Her voice was hoarse and rough from disuse, barely audible.

He reached for her hand. "Lie still, Aveleen. Matt wants to start an IV for you. Let him. We have a few hours to go. But you're safe. We have your notes as well that we'll give to Frankie."

She stared around at the men watching her, fear driving her questions. "Logan? Is he alive? I saw him run down."

Abe shared a look with Matt Cahill, the paramedic on his team, before he sighed. "He's okay from that, Aveleen, but he and Avery were looking for you. Someone went to shoot Avery and Logan took the bullet for him. He's still in the hospital, unconscious.

We'll get you to him as soon as we can." He watched with compassion as her eyes slid closed and tears trickled down her cheeks. She dozed off, Matt watching carefully for any signs that she was in distress.

Murphy tucked her close to him at the hospital, his arm around her supporting her as she walked slowly towards the building, her thoughts on Logan. She listened as he once again spoke about Logan's condition and what the doctors had said. She didn't realize the rest of Abe's men had surrounded the two of them, protecting them, putting their lives in danger to do just that. She paused at the room door, her hand on the handle, before she looked up, unable to articulate her thanks, seeing Murphy nod in understanding before he shoved the door open for her.

It was far from over, he knew. Abe had talked to them, asking for their help in protecting these two. Not one man had refused. Abe stood for a moment in the doorway, watching as Leigh turned, startled, towards the bed and then began to move towards Aveleen. Aveleen's focus was on Logan and saw no one else.

Aveleen came back to the present, her face soaked with sweat and tears, her hand clutching tightly to Logan's, before she looked at Frankie and nodded. He reached to turn off the dictator.

"I'll bring back the printed statement later today, Aveleen. Please don't speak with anyone until you have signed it. I know others will want to know what happened." He studied her face and arms. "I am also going to have one of the crime scene techs stop by. We need photographs of your injuries." At her protest, he shook his head. "If we don't, it will be your word against theirs that you were beaten. Your clothes? In the bathroom still? I need to take those as well."

He hesitated before he walked away, his thoughts dark, but his heart raising in prayer for his young friend and her husband. This wasn't over, he knew, but he wished it was. He prayed for healing for both, that Logan's injuries wouldn't be life changing after all.

Aveleen watched him walk away, knowing he'd be back and that he's have more questions. She had given him the combination to her safe and he said he'd find the packet she had there. She shivered with fear as she remembered the wording of the threats.

Turning back to Logan, she touched his face, finding herself calming down even with just that touch. She reached to kiss his cheek, feeling the roughness of the beard he had grown over the last few weeks. She sighed once more, knowing she wanted him to wake up, but knowing she didn't want him to see her looking like she did. When someone came in who she could ask a favour of, she would put in a request for some makeup, hoping to cover the worst of the bruising before he saw her.

Chapter 24

His eyes flickering open and closed, Logan was sure he heard Aveleen talking. But that couldn't be!   She was missing, wasn't she?   He gave a low groan and felt hands on his face and then his chest, holding him still.

"Logan, don't move.   Please!   Don't move.   Not until the surgeon has been in." Aveleen's hand on his face and chest didn't work.

Logan stirred, groaning louder. "Aveleen?   Is that you?"   He finally managed to open his eyes enough to squint around, seeing his beloved bride in his line of sight. "How?"

"Sssh.   Not now.   I'll explain.   I just need you to lie still. Please!"

"No, I need to get up.   I need to find Aveleen.   She's gone!" He tried to move his legs and couldn't and just didn't understand why they weren't working as they should.

"Logan!   Please!   Please stay still!" Aveleen was growing frantic, trying to hold

Logan still but finding him fighting her as best he could. She turned her head as she heard footsteps and saw the nurse approaching. "Please? He's awake, or sort of, and trying to get up."

The nurse took one look and was gone from the room, back in just a few minutes. "The surgeon's on the floor. He'll be in directly." She too tried to calm Logan but found it almost a losing battle until he sank back, his eyes closing from exhaustion.

"What happened, Aveleen?" The surgeon spoke from beside her even as he reached to begin his assessment of Logan.

"He woke up and tried to get out of the bed." Aveleen's voice was frantic with worry. "I tried to stop him but I couldn't. He was fighting me." She looked at Logan and then the surgeon. "What damage did he do?"

"I don't think he's done any." The surgeon rested his hand on the side rail of the bed and then spoke. "I'm not seeing the damage I would expect to see from the wound. He has sensation in his feet and legs and if there was a lot of damage he wouldn't. As to why he's not moving them, there is still swelling in the area, which may be the cause. It's a day to day process with him, Aveleen."

"Will it be like this every time he awakens? Will I have to fight him to keep him still?" Aveleen's concern was growing with each word she spoke.

"You may but then again you may not. We need you here now that he's waking up, but we can't have you forfeiting your own wellbeing. We will need to set boundaries for you both."

Aveleen shook her head, her hand going back to clasp Logan's. "That's not happening, Doctor. I am not leaving his side."

The surgeon sighed in frustration, knowing that was exactly what she would do, before he walked away, leaving new orders on Logan's chart.

Logan roused again later that day, his eyes fluttering open, feeling more sane than he had earlier. He searched the room, taking in the equipment still there, before his eyes lit on a head of black curls. He drew in a deep breath, closed his eyes and rubbed at them, before he opened them. Aveleen! You're here, he thought. But how?

He reached out a hand, not quite making it to touch hers before he tried to shift in bed, the pain from his back stopping him. He stared at his feet and legs, realizing that they hadn't moved with him. His head back on the pillow, his eyes focused on the ceiling, he tried to remember what had happened but couldn't.

Aveleen roused as she heard Logan moving and was on her feet at his side, her hand on his cheek.

"Logan? Are you awake? Really awake this time?" Her soft voice had him turning to her.

"Aveleen? You're really here? I'm not dreaming?"

"No, you're not dreaming. I really am here." She watched as his eyes slid closed and then popped open. "No, we're not talking about that right now. I can't. Frankie won't let me."

Logan just stared at her before he looked towards the end of the bed. "What happened to me, Aveleen? The last I remember is talking to Avery about where you might be."

"Apparently you two set out to try and find me. You saw someone about to shoot Avery and took Avery down, getting hit in the process." She blinked back tears. "The surgeon is still trying to determine just how bad you are."

"I can't move my legs, can I? How bad does it have to be before he knows?"

She rubbed his arm. "He doesn't think it's permanent. That he's told me. They've been waiting for you to wake up to do a proper assessment. He was in earlier today."

"Aveleen?" Logan waited until she looked at him, her eyes shadowed. "How did you get here? And how long have I been here?"

"Abe found me. I can't tell you how. Frankie isn't letting me talk about. To tell you the truth, I'm not quite sure myself." She looked behind her at the closed door. "Abe has some of his men outside right now. I just wish this was over."

"As do I." Logan reached for the bed rails, shifting his weight. "When can I get out of here?"

Neither heard the door open softly or the quiet footsteps as the surgeon approached once more. His appearance caused Aveleen to jump in fright and pale, Logan's hand reaching for hers.

"If you continue as you are, we'll send you to a rehab hospital in about a week or ten days." He frowned as Logan shook his head. "Logan, that's not an option. You need to go there."

"No, I don't. I can find someone to help me at home. What are they going to do for me there? Teach me to live in a wheelchair and maneuver around the hospital? That won't help me at home." His grip tightened on Aveleen's hand. "I just want to go home, Doc. That's all. When is that possible?"

The surgeon argued with him before finally throwing up his hands. "Let's see. You've just wakened up. Give me four or five days with you and the physiotherapist here. Then we'll talk."

"There will be no talking, Doc. Four days is all you get. Then I am wheeling myself out of here."

The surgeon just stared at him before shaking his head and walking away. Aveleen watched him go before she turned back to Logan, her mouth open to speak before she snapped it closed. She watched the emotions flittering across his face.

"We'll need to make the house handicap accessible, my love. Yours and mine both. Greg said he had offers to help us. I've told him to go ahead."

"Are you sure?" At her nod, he sighed. "I just wish we didn't have to. This is so frustrating, Sweetest. How do we go on from here?"

"In God, that's how." She slid down on the bed beside him, his arm around her, her head on his shoulder. "We'll get there, my love. Somehow, we'll get there. And we will get you back on your feet."

"I know, Sweetest thing in my life. It's just such a shock to wake up and find out I can't walk." He plucked at the blanket, staring at the IV line in his hand. "And you, Sweetest? You're okay?"

"Physically, I am getting there. It's every other emotion I'm trying to deal with. Greg has been by as has Emma. I've talked to them. Your Mom has been in and out. My parents and brothers have taken up residence I think in the waiting room." She turned to look at the door, sudden fear in her heart. "I'm just afraid, Logan." Her voice was barely a whisper.

"I know. That's when we have to pray the hardest, Aveleen. Pray for peace, for courage, for safety. The man is still out there, isn't he?"

She nodded. "I was finally able to give a name to Frankie, or names rather. I recognized them at last."

He nodded, his eyes closing as he drifted off to sleep. Aveleen watched him closely, seeing the fatigue and pain drawing lines into his beloved face, lines that she blamed herself for. She rose, stretched and headed for the waiting room, looking for someone she could talk to. Emma rose and came towards her, drawing her into a hug and then into an empty room, sitting her down, her arm around her friend and praying for her. Aveleen looked up finally, thanks on

235

her lips that died as she watched Emma closely.

"Emma?"

"Aveleen, I sense something about you that's different. What are you planning?"

Aveleen shrugged. "Nothing that I know of. Just trying to think of how we'll manage once Logan gets home. He's told the surgeon four days is all he'll stay."

"He's awake? Oh, praise the Lord! Now we can get him better."

"As long as it's better and not bitter. Oh, Emma! How do we go on? This isn't over. How did you ever do it for all those years, thinking Abe was dead?"

"God.   That's the only way I got through it. And I think there was a little part of me that refused to admit that Abe was dead, that was convinced my uncle was so wrong, that the pictures he showed me lied. And that little part of me was so right."

Aveleen's head tilted as she watched the older lady, knowing Emma had just bared her heart to her. "Thank you, Emma. I'm just so tired, I just want this over."

"Be careful what you are wishing for, Aveleen. That's my advice. It may be a lot worse before it's over. And just how are you feeling now?" Emma's eyes caught movement outside the door and watched as Murphy hesitated before he nodded and moved on.

"Abe's men are out there, aren't they? Don't they have an assignment or something they have to get to?"

Emma laughed at the disgruntled tone to her voice. "Right now, you and Logan are their assignment. Once you are home, they'll back off some."

"Yeah, right. Back off some, you say? That won't happen."

Emma's laughter rang through the room as she watched Aveleen struggle with her emotions before a smile crept across the younger woman's face.

"Did I really just say that?"

Chapter 25

Wheeling his chair up the ramp that had been built to his porch, Logan paused, the effort of doing just that exhausting him. Avery stood behind him, his hands clenching and unclenching as he wanted to help but knew he had to wait to be asked. Logan looked back at him and nodded.

"I could use some help, thanks, Avery." He sighed. This was not how he had planned their homecoming. Not by a long shot.

"Where to?"

"The bedroom." Aveleen stood just inside the door, a stern look on her face. "Just for a bit, my love. This moving home has exhausted you."

Logan finally nodded, acquiescing to her request. He knew if he didn't she would make it an order and he would have to do what she asked. He leaned on Avery as he slid to the bed, watching as Avery lifted his legs up and then stood back.

"Stop blaming yourself, Avery. We had no way of knowing someone was out there. He could have been gunning for either one of us."

"I know. It's just that it was me and you took the fall for me." He paused, blinking hard for a moment before he turned and almost ran from the room.

Aveleen watched him go before she approached Logan, helping him adjust the pillows behind his head and pulling a light blanket up over him. She sat beside him, her hand in his.

"You're home, my love. Now you can rest properly. No one does at the hospital."

"Aveleen, we need to talk at some point. I don't care what Frankie has told you. I need to know exactly what went on and who your abductors were. I can't heal if I don't know." Logan's hand rubbed up and down her arm, his eyes watching the shadows on her face. "It's hard, I know, Sweetest, but we'll get there."

"I know." She refused to look at him, her hand clenching and unclenching before she finally sighed and rose. "Do you want anything right now?"

"No, I'm fine." He watched as she paced the bedroom before he reached for her hand as she passed the bed, pulling her back down beside him. "Aveleen, don't hide anything from me. Please? I know you have been."

She finally gave a nod. "I won't. Not any more. But I don't think this could have been prevented, Logan. Not even if we had never married."

"I know that." He shifted as best he could, glaring at his legs. "I feel so helpless. How am I to protect you, when I'm like this?"

"You're not. That's God's job." She leaned towards him as he reached to wrap her in his arms. "I'm so scared, Logan. I am just so scared." She swallowed hard, not sure how to proceed. "I didn't tell you. I couldn't." She paused again, unable to continue.

"Who did they threaten, Aveleen? Who?"

"All of us. They've even threatened the baby. I can't let anything happen to her, Logan. How can I? But how do I stop them?"

Logan's arms tightened around her. "We figure it out, Sweetest. Somehow, we'll figure it all out."

Logan began to pray as he had never prayed before. He knew God would protect them, would only allow what was in His will for them, but he was scared for Aveleen, and yes, he had to admit it, for the rest of their families. He raised his eyes to his wife's face, seeing the stress there. How did he go on, he wondered?

Aveleen finally raised up, watching as Logan slept. She was tired herself, no, exhausted, but there were things she had to do. She moved silently through the house, checking on the security upgrades Abe had insisted on before she stepped out into the backyard. She sighed. This could be so much an oasis, if things were different. She liked the gardens already there but she could see where she could change things around, remove plantings and add her own. Logan wouldn't care, that much she knew. If it made her happy, he would be all for it. She wandered the yard for a while before heading back inside, shivering in the cool air, but not from that. She felt watched. The eyes everyone had described in their adventure were out there, trained on her. How did she ever escape from them? God, are You even there? Do you even care about us? Why, Lord? Why us?

She stopped in the kitchen, thinking to prepare a meal, when the doorbell rang. She groaned. Please, Lord. No visitors. I can't handle that.

She peeked through the window. Greg and his wife, Mary, stood there. She couldn't avoid them, now could she? She pulled the door open, trying to compose her face, trying to come up with words of welcome as they stepped through. Mary took one look at her, handed Greg the dish she held and swept the younger woman into her arms, her hug tight around Aveleen as Aveleen wept. Greg looked around, heading for the kitchen, and then quietly through the house, seeking to find what he could do to help. He paused as he heard Logan's voice and stepped to the doorway of the bedroom.

Logan looked up, surprised to see Greg, but welcoming his assistance back to his chair. Frustration grew within him. This is not how he had pictured his life.

"Logan? It's okay. I can take what you dish out. Do you need to cry? Do you need to yell, scream, vent, rage? Get mad at God?   Tell Him off and then ask for forgiveness?" Greg sat across from Logan the living room, his words startling the younger man.

"How did you know?" Logan shook his head. "Forget I asked that."

"It's okay. I had a grandfather who was a paraplegic. I used to help him when he needed it. He was a proud man, not liking to ask for help."

Logan nodded, seeing where Greg was heading with that. "You're telling me not to be too proud, to ask for help if I need it."

Greg grinned. "I knew I liked you for a reason, Logan. You're a smart man and a quick learner. Now, about your columns? I hear they've become very popular."

"That they have. I am surprised at how popular.   My old publisher called yesterday, asking how I was and letting me know that the columns have been picked up by more papers. Something about being a modern-day pioneer is resounding with the people or some such nonsense." Logan grinned for a moment, his thoughts on his work. "I have so much to share, that I just can't get the words down fast enough." He stared down at his legs. "At least that's something I can do while I'm stuck in here." He looked around for a moment, not seeing Aveleen. "How is Aveleen from your standpoint?"

Greg sighed, having expected that very question. "She's hurting, Logan. She's changed from what we all knew. Some for the good, but also it has changed her in a way none of us like to see. Your being in her life is helping. She can depend on you." He held up a hand when Logan went to protest. "I don't care about your handicap right now, Logan. I know it's a big thing in your life and you're trying to cope with that and come to an understanding as to why and how your life goes on. I understand from Aveleen that it might not be permanent, but that's not a given either. As to Aveleen, she's strong, stronger than any of us have expected her to be. She kept a lot of herself hidden, for reasons we don't know and we didn't ask. She's a private person that way."

"She is, but she is talking more and more with me, telling me things that she has never told anyone else. Aubrey's talked to me as well, as has Holly. The one who seems to know her best is Avery. And he's not saying much. I have no idea what happened between the two of them, but something drastic did. It was before she was abducted the first time. He started to say something when we were out searching for her, but stopped himself. He said I'd have to ask Aveleen. I haven't had the heart to approach her yet." He looked up as he heard footsteps heading their way. "Who's with Aveleen?"

"Mary is. She wanted to come by, bring you a meal. The church ladies have organized a list to bring you your main meals for the next week or ten days." Greg grinned at the look on Logan's face. "Don't protest, Logan. Just accept that the ladies feel this is one way to serve God. You can use it for fodder in one of your columns."

Logan stared at him for a moment before he grinned and then shook a finger at him. "Don't give me any ideas. It just might happen."

"What might happen?" Aveleen stopped beside Logan, her hand on his shoulder, giving a slight squeak as he wrapped an arm around her and pulled her down onto his lap, blushing as he did so.

"That I will use the church ladies' service to us in a column. Now, Mary, I understand you have brought us a meal. Join us, please?"

Chapter 26

The days passed slowly, or so it seemed afterwards to Aveleen. She paced the house at any hour of the day or night, rising during the night to do so, waiting until she was certain Logan was asleep and then seeking her rest once more before she thought he would awaken, snuggling close to him, trying to find her peace again that he helped her to find, taking comfort in his strong arm around her. She didn't know that he roused when she left and didn't sleep again until she was back beside him. His heart raised in prayer during those hours, seeking the Lord's comfort and peace and will, raging at Him at times, questioning, railing against Him, but always coming back to asking for peace, for patience, for comfort, for safety.

Logan watched as Aveleen lost weight, grew pale and quiet. He missed the spark that she had begun to show before her second abduction. Whatever had happened to her had almost destroyed her, had broken her, he thought. How did she heal was his daily question, and his daily prayer for just that. He would sit for long periods of time, his eyes on his legs, willing them to move, but finding they just didn't. He sighed at long last, resigning himself to the fact that he would never likely walk again, although the surgeon had told him that the healing from the bullet wound was good, that the nerves were knitting back together, and that there was no reason he couldn't walk. Was it because he didn't want to, he was asked. He had grown angry at that very question and had turned his chair and wheeled away as quickly as he could. He never told Aveleen what he had been asked, knowing if he did, she would ask him why not.

He didn't know how many times Aveleen had walked the outside of the house, searching for anything that shouldn't be there, finding envelopes with threats and pictures that she didn't look at, simply handed to Frankie without a word. Frankie would open them, go to ask her about them, and then stop, seeing the shuttered look on her face. He knew something had been said or done with the last abduction that had broken her. He had seen it before. He sighed, and had gone to a friend's wife, who was a psychologist, and talked to her, seeking to find answers or ways he could help his two friends.

Aveleen knew she should talk to Logan, but somehow she just couldn't open up.   The threats that had broken her resounded in her mind. How could she tell him? But then again, how could she not? She was torn and found him watching her at times without a word.

Abe had been around, asking if she had seen anyone. She had shook her head, and he had just given her that look he knew how to give. She had told him to talk to Frankie, that he had the threats and photos, that she hadn't seen them, and neither had Logan. In fact, she was adamant that Logan not be told. The last time she told him that, Abe had stared at her before looking behind her at Logan on the front porch, watching closely, and bluntly told her she was wrong, that she was doing Logan a disservice and he needed to be told. It didn't matter he was in a wheelchair, he was her husband and at risk. How could he be prepared if she kept him in the dark? She had finally nodded, agreeing that she needed to talk to him, but she wasn't sure just how to. Abe had wrapped her in a hug and then arm around her shoulder, led her back to the porch, sitting her down. He waited for her to speak and when she didn't, he spoke for her.

Logan had stared first at Abe and then turned to Aveleen, his arms reaching to draw her to him, his cheek resting against her head. He felt the shudders of fear, no, terror, he thought, running through her.

"Aveleen? What else haven't you told me?" He waited, his eyes on Abe, who in turn watching the younger couple closely.

"I'm sorry, Logan. I just couldn't. I am not sure even now that I should have let Abe speak."

"He had to, Aveleen. I needed to know. I know why you didn't, that you wanted to protect me. But, Sweetest, not telling isn't protecting me. It's protecting the man behind this." He paused as she stiffened. "Aveleen? What is it?"

She leaned back to look up at him, shaking her head, unable to articulate what she needed to say.

"What, Sweetest?   The man?   You can't tell me who is it?" He paused at the look crossing her face. "What is it?"

"He's not the leader.   I am not sure who it is, but it's not him." She looked up, blinking against the memory, her hand tightening on Logan's. "He's not the leader. I think I know who it is and it's frightening."

Abe leaned forward.   "You gave the name of the man to Frankie, didn't you?" When she shook her head, he groaned. "Aveleen?   You didn't?   How could you not?"

"Because he threatened Holly's baby. He said he would either take her away forever or kill her. I can't let him do that." She refused to look at Abe, fear and distress on her face, breaking the men's hearts as they watched her.

"But, Aveleen, keeping quiet isn't protecting her. He can strike at any time, for any reason." Abe shared a look with Logan. "Tell me, please. Who is it?"

She shivered, her mouth opening and closing before she finally said a name, a name that had Abe sitting back abruptly in his chair, his eyes narrowing.

"Him? He's the one?" At her nod, he drew a deep breath. "Okay. This is what we'll do. I'll have Emma or Jace research him. Then we'll give the name to Frankie or Caleb." He watched as she paled even more. "It has to be done, Aveleen. Now, you said he's not the one in charge. Do you have any suspicion as to who it is?"

She nodded. "I do, but I can't prove it." She looked at Abe, her heart on her face. "You know her too, Abe." When she spoke the name, he paled. "See? How can I accuse her without proof?"

"We'll find the proof, Aveleen. That I promise you. Knowing Emma and Jace, this will become a priority for them."

"Oh, no!" Aveleen grew visibly upset. "They can't set everything aside for this."

"But they will. They want this over for you two as well."

They watched as Abe finally rose and walked away, promising to be back the next day. Logan's arms tightened around his bride, not letting her push herself away from him.

"Logan?" Her voice was so soft he barely heard her speak.

"Oh, Sweetest. Is this why you've been pacing all the time?" At her nod, he sighed, a prayer going up. "Don't stay quiet, please? Talk to me?"

She agreed, albeit reluctantly and finally rose and walked away from him, heading for their office, and to her work. She didn't start for a while, her mind blank, not wanting to think. She didn't hear him stop his chair at the doorway to watch before he moved on.

Chapter 27

Aveleen watched from the front porch the next morning as Abe walked the perimeter of their yard, Logan sitting on the front walk, his eyes on their friend. She sighed. Now that she had said the two names, she was ever more terrified, if that was at all possible. She shuddered at the remembered threats, the threats of harm and death that had been spewed at her that last day before she was locked into the mine. She knew Abe had talked to Holly and Lincoln and had them hidden somewhere safe, until they could find the man responsible for her abductions and the woman behind him. She was thankful Abe had believed her, had not questioned her as to why she had refused to say anything.

Logan shifted in his chair, his eyes seeking her, and she walked down the ramp to stand beside him, her arm around his shoulder, his around her waist, pulling her tight to him. They knew they were being watched, but couldn't see anyone.

Abe looked grim as he walked back across the lawn, his eyes on the tree across the street.

"Abe?" Aveleen's voice was quiet as she spoke.

"There are cameras pointing at the doors and windows, Aveleen. I've found a number, including in the tree across the street. Frankie is on his way with techs to remove them." He sighed. "This just doesn't stop for you. Let me go through the house. I doubt they've made their way inside but I want to be sure." He paused, sharing a look with Logan, before shaking his head and moving away from them.

Frankie stood for a moment, watching as the techs worked away before he approached Aveleen, who was by now seated in the swing on the back deck. He sat beside her, his foot pushing at the floor to start the swing moving.

"Aren't you going to tell me off, Frankie?"

Aveleen's voice was too quiet, Frankie thought. She's subdued, and that's not her. No, he thought, she has been since the first abduction. I want my vibrant friend back, Lord, and I don't think that will happen.

"No, why would I? You have now. That's the main thing. You didn't know when you were rescued the first time. He's made you so afraid that you don't want to talk about it. But you need to. Talk to Darcie. She's willing to help you, to talk to you."

She nodded. "I might, but I don't want to impose on a friend."

Frankie's hand reached to squeeze hers. "She wants you to. That's what she's said."

Logan paused in the doorway before he wheeled towards them. "Frankie? Can you say what you've found so far?"

"A number of cameras. That's it. No microphones or anything like that. Abe didn't find anything in the house, which we're thankful for." Frankie shot a look towards the back of the yard. "Having the trees back there have sheltered you but it's also provided a way for him to move in and out. Have you thought about getting a dog?"

Aveleen shook her head. "No. No dog. I can't." She was up and in the house before Logan could ask why.

Logan's eyes followed her before he turned a stern look at Frankie. "What was that all about?"

"She was bitten as a young child by a small dog. An ankle biter, if I recall. She's never liked dogs since then and in fact, goes out of her way to avoid them."

Logan sighed. "I guess there goes that plan."

"What plan?"

"I was going to get her a puppy for her birthday in two weeks."

Frankie shook his head. "I wouldn't, if I were you. Maybe a cat?" He laughed at the look on Logan's face. "No? No cat?"

"I'm not real fond of them, but if it works for Aveleen, then I would say yes. Why? Do you have one you're trying to get rid of?"

"Deirdre's cousin found some kittens near the shelter. One little calico girl is a sweetheart. She'd help heal Aveleen's heart, I think."

"Let me think about that. I want to talk to her first."

Abe stood for a moment, watching the two men. "Frankie? Did you get everything?"

Frankie nodded. "I believe we did. We found a dozen in total. Now, those names you promised me?"

Abe sighed. "I thought there were more. Thank you. As for the names, here." He handed his friend a folder. "Emma and Jace have been doing some work. You know how thorough they are. This is what they've found so far."

Frankie took a look at the stack of papers in the folder before looking at Logan. "Logan doesn't know your wife and how she works. Logan, this will just be the beginning. Emma will keep at it, giving us what we need to investigate."

"That she will. Where's Aveleen?" Abe looked around for her.

"In the house. Do you need her?" Logan moved his hands to the wheels, ready to go and find her.

"No, it's not important. I'll be back later." Abe walked away, hands jammed into his jacket pockets.

"Abe's up to something, Logan. I can tell you that much." Frankie knew his friend well.

"I suspected that." He watched Frankie for a moment. "And so are you. Care to share with me?"

Frankie stared at him for a moment before he grinned. "No, not really. We're still working through some issues." He paused as his phone chimed and he glanced down at the text. "Well, well. Now that's what I like to hear." He looked up, seeing Aveleen standing in front of him. "Aveleen. Just the lady I wanted to see."

"And why would that be?" She slid back onto the swing, her hand reaching for Logan's. She somehow knew something big had happened.

"The detectives have just brought in a couple of young men, both under 18. They're connected to the name you gave us."

She paled and began to shake her head. "No, Frankie. No! He'll come looking for me. There's no question about that. He'll believe I turned them in."

"He can't. They were arrested for a break and enter, not connected to you. At least not yet. We'll be talking to them once they have their lawyers in place." He rose, his eyes on his friends. "I'll call later with an update."

Aveleen sat for a while, her arms wrapped around herself. She didn't respond when Logan spoke to her. He finally moved away, back to the office, and lost himself to his columns. He didn't hear Aveleen moving around until she spoke to him.

"Logan?"

He looked up, blinked, and then smiled at her. "Aveleen? How long have you been there?"

"Not very long. You were totally into your work." She walked over and perched on the corner of his desk. "How are your columns?"

"I have enough done now for a couple of weeks." He sat back, his eyes assessing her. "Why?"

She shrugged. "I just wondered. It feels like we're just in a holding pattern, that something drastic is about to happen, and I don't want it to."

He nodded. "I know that feeling. I've felt it before." He rubbed at his chest.

"Logan? When did you get that scar?"

"The scar? When I was just starting college. I had a part-time job working for a local paper and had gone to interview an older gentleman. Only it was a set up. I didn't trust my instincts in time and ended up with a knife wound. Not deep but deep enough that it left the scar. I've been more careful since then."

She watched him for a moment. "Have you been? Really and truly?"

He sighed, knowing what she was asking. "I have tried, Aveleen. Sometimes, circumstances are beyond our control. That's what we facing right now. Only God has control of it. He is there, whether you believe it or not."

"I'm having trouble doing just that." Her face was troubled. "I don't like doubting God or not trusting but that's what I feel like I am doing."

"He knows and understands. That I do know. He cares deeply for you, Aveleen. Never lose sight of that."

She nodded once more. "I get that in my head. My heart is another story." She rose and began to pace. "I just feel like the next week will be it." She spun as he made a sound. "Logan?"

"I think I agree. They're not going to let it go on forever. That much is a given."

Chapter 28

Logan shoved the door open to the back deck a few days later, wheeling outside and then down the ramp to the patio area where he sat, his thoughts dark. Frankie had just called.   The two young men hadn't spoken, had just smirked when questioned. They were still in jail, awaiting an arraignment before a judge. Charges related to Aveleen were before the judge as well, but Frankie said there was no guarantee they'd be kept in jail.   He suggested that Logan and Aveleen find somewhere to hide for the next few weeks.

He knew before he even talked to Aveleen what her response would be. She had told him at breakfast that morning that she wouldn't run, wouldn't hide. She was tired of even thinking about that.   He had watched her face, seeing the fear lurking in her eyes but also the determination to find the young man responsible for her beatings and then the woman behind him. When he questioned as to how she planned to stay safe, she had just shrugged. He could feel the anger growing inside him and this time no prayers were working. He could not quench that fire burning.

He stared down at the plastic water bottle he held and then at his useless legs as he termed them. He could feel the prickles in his back, the pins and needles sensations but ignored them. He didn't think he would ever walk again and that helped to fuel his anger. Why, God? He questioned daily, why him. Then he would change the question to why not him. He turned slightly as he heard a noise but didn't see anything. He spun his chair to stare down the yard, wanting to walk the yard, to see what Aveleen had been doing in the gardens, knowing she was pulling weeds and annual plants, readying them for the colder months.

He stared once more at the water bottle before his arm came back and he hurled it at the tree near the house, watching as it slammed into the trunk and exploded, water flying everywhere. He froze as he heard a slight sound and turned, seeing Aveleen standing there, hands to her cheeks, a look of horror on her face before she spun and ran back into the house, the door slamming behind her.

"Aveleen?" He groaned even as he shoved his hands against the chair wheels, moving as quickly as he could up the ramp. "Aveleen? Sweetest?"

He struggled to open the door, frustration at not being able to get to his bride in his actions. He wheeled through the house, finding her crumpled in a heap in the office. He paused, then wheeled towards her, reaching to pull her to her feet. She refused to move. He sighed, and then levered himself forward enough that he could slide to the floor beside her, his arm around her, his head bent over hers as he murmured his words of contrition and love. He was finally able to move her enough that both arms could surround her and he could pull her up onto his legs and cuddle her close to him.

His head against her, he held her, his tears damping her hair. He felt the tremors shaking her body and felt the anger that had burned within him seeping away.

"Aveleen? I'm sorry. I'm so sorry. I'm sorry, Sweetest. I didn't know you were there. I'm sorry." He waited for her to respond but she didn't. It's like she shut down, he thought. Lord, what did I do? How do I reach her?

He heard the front doorbell but refused to move, knowing that whoever was there would leave eventually. Then he heard the back door and a low voice calling for him. Abe? What was he doing here? He had forgotten Abe said he would be by about this time that morning.

Abe stood for a moment, studying Logan and Aveleen before he walked quietly across the room to sink to the floor near them, his eyes on Aveleen.

"Logan? What happened?"

Logan sighed, his eyes on Abe before they dropped to watch Aveleen. "I lost my temper, threw a water bottle at the tree out back. Aveleen saw me and ran. This is how I found her."

Abe nodded. "Fear. Terror. Shock. Whatever emotions she's been hiding just surfaced. A friend said to watch for this. She expected it long before this." He leaned back on his hands, still watching Aveleen. "How be we pack you two up and take you to our place? The cabin is available. We have men in for security training but the cabin I would use for you two is next to our house, among the houses my men have. It might do her good to get away from here." He looked around before he pulled out his phone and sent a quick text message. "I just sent a message to Murphy. He's been really concerned about you two. His wife will prepare the cabin. What can I do for you two right now?"

Logan sighed, knowing Abe was right. They needed to get away, but he wouldn't do that without Aveleen's agreement. "I need her to tell me it's what she'll do. I won't force her to go, Abe. I can't, not given what's happened to her." He paused, biting at his lip. "I love her too much to do that."

Aveleen stirred, catching Logan's last words, her head moving so she could watch his face, seeing the concern for her written on it. "Logan? What happened?"

He looked down at her, his arms tightening. "Frankie called. He thinks the youths will be out today. I am that worried about you. And yes, angry. That anger came out. It shouldn't have."

"No, it's okay, Logan. I have to learn to deal with my fear. It's not your fault."

She felt herself calming as she always did with his touch. She looked over, startled to see Abe sitting in front of her. "Abe? What are you doing here?"

"Talking with Logan?" He grinned as she shook her head at him. "I came to check in on you two. I have suggested to Logan that you two move out to Rebel's for now." He was referring to the compound or village as it had become where he lived.

She began to shake her head before she felt Logan's arm tighten on her and she turned to watch him again. "Logan? You think we should?"

"I think so, but I want what's best for you. If hiding isn't it, then we stay put. If we need to go away for a few days, then we do. But it's not a decision I want to make on my own. That's not fair to you. I love you too much to run roughshod over your wishes."

She finally shoved against him and stood, towering over him for a moment before she reached for his chair and then to help him up. Abe stood, ready to help, but amazed at how the two worked together to get Logan up and into his chair. He frowned, seeing movement from Logan's legs that hadn't been there a few days ago. Lord, is he healing? I pray he is.

Logan shifted to a more comfortable position in his chair before he wheeled towards the desk. "Abe, for now, I think we'll stay here. Unless and until Aveleen says otherwise." He watched as she paced before she turned, her mouth opening to speak before she snapped it closed. "Aveleen? You were about to say?"

She shrugged, her arms wrapping around her abdomen, a distressed, lost look on her face. "How can we leave, Logan? This is our home. It's all set up for you. Somewhere else won't be." She paused as she saw movement from Abe. "Abe? What have you gone and done?"

"Something Murphy and I have talked about for years. You know we've renovated the cabins into homes as each one of the team married and then began to have families. We realized that we needed to update all the cabins. That means changing door width, making things more accessible. The cabin we would put you in we decided would be a handicap accessible one. It's yours when you want it."

Her eyes on Logan, she hesitated, knowing what the men were asking of her. It would not be running and hiding. It would be a time that she and Logan could step away from what had happened and just be with one another. To have healing and restoration in their lives. She chewed at her lip, catching the grin Logan was trying hard to hide. He had read her correctly, she thought.

"Who's around this week?" Her question caught Abe's attention.

He knew she was more comfortable with some of the ladies, although she was friends with them all. "Let's see. Nathaniel's Elizabeth, Micah's Kataleen, Murphy's Adriel. The other ladies, including Rachel and Rebecca, are away at a conference of some kind." He knew the ladies he had just mentioned were dear to Aveleen's heart, even though they were a few years older than she was.

She stared at Logan, knowing he wouldn't make the decision but that he would back whatever she said, without question. She also knew if he felt strongly about it, he would just pack her up and take her away, if it meant her life. She sighed to herself. That's what it is, isn't it, Lord? A matter of life and death, and not just mine. Not any more. I'm not in this alone. She finally nodded, moving past the two men.

"I'll pack some things. Only for a few days, Abe. No more than a week is what I'll give you. Then, things change."

"Aveleen? Just what do you mean?" Abe's hand on her arm stopped her. He had a good idea what she was up to. "Don't put yourself out there."

"How else do I stop them, Abe? They're hiding and will continue to hide, taunting me, threatening our families." She shared a look with Logan. "Lincoln and Holly have no life. They're hiding because of me. Logan's parents and sister can't come see him. Mine have to stay away. Caleb's Hannah is almost ready to be put in hiding. Where do we stop?"

"Give me a couple of days to come up with a plan. That's all I ask. I know Murphy's been working on something. He's hurting for you, Aveleen."

She snorted at that. "Well, he shouldn't be. I've told him he's in the wrong line of work. His heart is too tender."

Abe laughed at her comment. "He told me and at the time wondered if you were right but decided that no, God had put him where he was needed most."

She finally walked away and they could hear her movements from the bedroom, the opening of the closet door, the opening and closing of dresser drawers. Logan sighed. This was not what he wanted. She was doing it because she was asked to, not because she felt it was the right thing to do. They had talked over various scenarios and what they should or shouldn't do. This was not one they had spent time over.

Abe moved away, heading outside, his phone to his ear. Logan watched him walk away before he turned to his desk, finding the cases for their laptops, wheeling to the door to set them the antique dresser used as a table in the entryway. He heard Aveleen approaching and turned, seeing the devastation of her face before she tried to clear it away. He reached for the bags she held, dropping them to the floor before he reached for her, pulling her to him, a kiss on the scar on her cheek, before he spoke.

"We don't have to do this, Aveleen. We can stay here. We can go somewhere else. I don't want to force you to do something you really don't want to."

She nodded, a sober look on her face. "It's not that I don't want to. I'm just not sure if this is the right step. Did I really agree to go to Rebel's?"

"You did. But we don't have to. I can call Abe back in here and tell him we're not going."

She shook her head. "For a few days. We need to make plans, Logan. I'm done running. Let's take a few days to try and agree on what we want to do. We both want this over and neither of us are talking about how to do just that."

Logan paused, thinking back over their conversations. "You're right. We've talked about so many other things, we skirted around this issue. Just know how much I love you. Whatever we decide, I want to make sure you are safe."

"I love you too, Logan but this is no life. We're living in fear each and every day as are our families. We need to end this." She rose from where she had been kneeling, opening the door before she reached back for their bags and headed towards her car, knowing Logan would lock up and follow her.

Logan wheeled towards the car, stopping for a moment to spin and stare back at their home, regret in his heart. This was no way to be starting a marriage, is it, Lord? But Aveleen's friends have had to do just that. All that I have met, except for Caleb and Hannah, and Greg and Mary, and if they had to, they're not talking. He turned back towards Aveleen once more, a flash of light catching his eye. He spun in a circle, not seeing the light again.

Abe had watched Logan's reaction and spun around himself. Someone was there, he knew that much. It was a given that someone would be watching them. Lord, help us keep this modern-day pioneer and his lady safe. It would break us if one of them died, and both have been so close.

Chapter 29

Watching as Aveleen seemed to relax with the ladies of Abe's team and with Abe's sister, Rebecca, Logan felt a sense of peace, at least for the moment. He turned and wheeled himself back to the cabin, knowing he needed to spend some time in prayer. He was growing bitter and angry and needed to deal with that. His hands stopped the wheels on his chair as he saw Murphy sitting on the porch rail, his eyes trained on the hills around the compound.

"Murphy?"

Murphy finally turned to him, a thoughtful look on his face. "Where's Aveleen?"

"With the ladies. I think there was talk of a party of some kind. She thought the ladies were all away but apparently changed their plans for her." Logan grinned, lighthearted for a moment. "She needs this time. She needs to forget for a few hours." He frowned, seeing something in Murphy's eyes. "But that's not why you're here."

Murphy drew a deep breath, not wanting to be the one to talk to Logan, but being told he had to be the one. He was the one who had carried Aveleen from the mine, had seen something that she had never been told, and that Logan needed to know what actually happened.

"Logan, we need to talk and we need to talk somewhere Aveleen's not about to walk in on us. It's going to be a long conversation. Matt has asked to join us, if that's okay with you." Murphy's voice was hesitant, not quite sure how to word what he needed to say.

"Well, sure, I guess. Where?" Logan turned his chair, ready to head into the house when Murphy's hand on the back of it stopped him. "Murphy?"

"Why don't we head to our office and use the meeting room there? That way, if we need to use a computer we can."

"And you think we'll have to?" Logan shook his head. "I don't like that look, Murphy. It's that bad?"

"It is. And it involves what happened to Aveleen that last time she was abducted." Murphy slowed his steps to walk alongside

Logan, seeing Matt waiting outside the office, hesitation in his stance, totally not typical for him.

Logan hesitated for a moment in the room door before he wheeled over to the table. He was tired of doing just that, of not being able to walk. He was growing bitter, he thought, and needed to work on that. Aveleen didn't deserve him that way.

Matt slid a mug of tea in front of him before he pulled out the chair beside him and sat, a file folder on the tabletop in front of him. Murphy slid into a chair as well, his eyes on a folder he had laid down before he looked up, pain briefly flickering across his face.

"Before we start, Logan, can we pray? Pray for you? Pray for Aveleen? Pray for whatever you'll be facing? That God will go before you and show Himself to you two?" At Logan's look of surprise, he gave a brief smile. "It's how we start our meetings, Logan. We pray for each other and our families and then for whatever situation we facing. It's the only way we've had the safety and protection we have had over the years."

Matt spoke up. "It's true, Logan. We know other teams that don't do that. The teams fracture. Men and women are hurt or killed. The situations they face go bad and go bad quickly."

Logan went to speak, and then couldn't, just bowing his head in response. He listened as the two men with him prayed, bringing him he felt right to the foot of God's throne in a way he had never experienced. Lord, I want this. I want this kind of relationship with you. Now. Not later. Not when things are changed. Not if I walk again. Just you and me, God. A Father and his son. Please, Lord?

He furtively wiped at his eyes, not catching the look Murphy and Matt shared before Matt spoke.

"How much have you been told, Logan? About her second abduction and how we found her?"

Logan shook his head. "I haven't been told anything other than that your team found her and brought her back to me. I know she was beaten severely. The bruises on her showed me that. I guess everyone thought I was too sick myself to hear anything."

"And you were, you know. You checked out of the hospital against medical advice, you know. They wanted you there for at least another week." Matt shook his head as he remembered the words that had been shared among his team members.

"I couldn't stay any longer. It was too hard on Aveleen. I guess I should have, but I couldn't." The stress from that time sounded in his voice once more.

"We get that, Logan. We've done the same ourselves." Murphy sipped at his water, not sure how to proceed. Matt looked at him and then spoke.

"Logan, this is going to be difficult for you to hear. It's difficult for us to talk about. Time has not dulled the memories. If you can let us talk and then ask questions, it will help." At Logan's nod of understanding, Matt continued. "You know we had been looking for her. We had word from someone, and we have not been able to determine exactly who it was. We think it was one of the youths working for the abductor. Anyway, we searched the buildings he said she was in and didn't find her. However, we did find some paperwork that had been dropped. It contained documented plans of how to abduct her, when to do so, where to take her, what was to happen to her if she refused to give them what they were asking for. That led us on a trail of trying to track where she was. Joseph finally cracked the list of places and with Micah found the mine. It is an abandoned one deep in another county. One that we would never have found. We should not have found it. When we got there, we found her and Murphy brought her out."

Murphy shook his head at Matt. "Matt hasn't said it all. When we finally reached the mine, we didn't see the men around. But there was a young boy, around 11 he told us. He was to watch from the shadows, take pictures of who showed up, and then send them on to a number. We tried to track that number but it wasn't active by then. He had hidden himself well. It's just we're used to doing that, finding people hiding. Joseph and Abe stayed with him. Luke, Matt and I went in to find Aveleen. We searched for a full hour before we found the new boards on the dead end of a tunnel. It took some work to pull them off. Matt here checked Aveleen out enough that we could move her. I carried her out, Matt and Luke watching for us.

"She roused briefly a few times, but not long enough for us to tell her where we found her or what had happened to you. That Abe did when we were about half-way here. I had to tell her again when I walked her into the hospital. She refused to have anyone look at her, just wanted to find you. That's all that mattered to her."

Murphy paused, seeing the distress on Logan's face, his heart breaking for his friend. "Logan, there was nothing you could have done to stop this. If they hadn't taken her that day, they would have found her. If they had found the two of you together, you would have been killed. That much we know from the notes we found. They have no respect for any life. To these young men, it's a game. It's like they are living in a video game, losing sight of reality."

Logan finally broke his silent, his voice torn with the stress of what he had just been told. "How bad was it?"

"Was what? Where we found her?" At his nod, Matt shared a look with Murphy. "It was bad, Logan. There was water dripping into the shaft. A good rain would have flooded the area. That had happened we could tell from the walls. There was no way she could have gotten out of that area. They used large spikes to nail the boards to the frame. With the beating she had taken, given the dampness and cold in that area, she would not have lasted more than twenty four hours. At the most."

Logan's head dropped as he listened to Matt. He knew it had been close for her but didn't realize just how close. "I didn't know, Matt. Murphy. No one told me. Aveleen won't talk about that last abduction. She said she gave Frankie her statement but said she told him she wouldn't talk about it with anyone. I can't get her to tell me anything." He drew a shaky breath. "How do we protect her now?"

"That's why you're here. Abe pushed and knew she would resist. We need to make plans. If we can set some in place and then let her know we have worked them out, she may agree."

Logan snorted. "You don't know her. She'll never agree. Not now. She's at the point she's ready to go looking for the culprits herself." He paused, his gaze on his hands. "She's changed, guys. She's not the person you knew. Not anymore. I hate that she's changed so much."

The two men with him nodded. "We get that, Logan." Murphy spoke up. "But we need to keep her safe, even if she fights us."

Logan pushed back from the table. "I know you've made plans. Let me say something before you go ahead with telling me." He paused, gathering his thoughts, his eyes on his hands. "I want to protect her at any cost, even my own life. She's not happy with that. She'll never agree to being put away, being kept out of the loop as they say. I know she's been researching the names she gave to Frankie. And I know who they are but it's not for me to say. You may have been given them but I won't break Aveleen's trust in me to go behind her back. Now, she has agreed to stay here until Saturday. That's three days from now. At that point, we move home, whether to my house or hers, we're still talking about that. I know

283

your team means well and I thank you for going ahead with this. Let me approach her again. She may change her mind but if she doesn't, we step back and wait for her leading. That's how it will have to be." He spun his chair and wheeled away, leaving Matt and Murphy staring after him before they shared a look.

Chapter 30

Aveleen watched Logan carefully, as he sat, his arms resting on the table, the newspaper in front of him, but she knew he was not reading. He was lost in thought. Her hand trailing across his shoulders, she pulled out a chair and then sat beside him, her head on her hand as she watched him.

"Logan? What did Murphy and Matt want?"

He looked up, not surprised that she knew but curious as to how she did. "How did you know?"

"Sarah. She went to say something and then stopped. So I knew they were up to something. What did they tell you?"

He sighed, pushing away the paper and turning to face her, reaching for her hands. "Aveleen, I didn't agree with speaking behind your back but they felt I needed to know how you were found and how they found you. They told me you have refused to talk about it."

She nodded, her face pensive. "I have, my love. Part of it is fear. They drove it into me with every blow I took that if I talked someone I loved would be hurt. I couldn't do that to anyone."

"But in keeping quiet, who were you protecting?"

She started at his question, remembering that he had asked that before. "I'm sorry, Logan. I guess I was trying to protect you and everyone else but that's not what happened, is it?"

He reached to pull her to him, his arms strong around her. "Now, we have to make some decisions. I know you want to go out there and find them. We can do that, but we need to make plans before we do." He reached under his paper and handed her a sheet that he had printed. "Here. My publisher has agreed to run this column. We just need to work it over and make sure it says what we want."

She froze, her eyes on him before they dropped to the paper. "Logan, just what did you go and do?"

"I wrote a column, directed at the abductors and whoever is behind them. The publisher of the newspaper in town wants it. He wants this all over for you as well."

She stared at him for a while. "Are you sure? This is really putting it out there."

He nodded. "I have to do what I can. I can't walk around and find them. This may bring them out." He watched as a shuttered look fell over her face. "Aveleen, I have talked to Caleb. I have talked to Frankie. I have talked to Dougal. I have talked to Abe. I talked to your Dad, my Dad, Lincoln, Aubrey and Avery. They don't like it, but they understand why we would take this step. It's not something I have entered into lightly. But know this. This column will not go into any paper until and unless you agree with it. That's a given. I won't put you out there without your consent and agreement to this step."

She sighed, the sigh drawn from deep within her before she read the column, her face paling as she did so. "Logan? Are you sure?"

"I am. But are you? It's your life at stake, Sweetest."

She nodded, then reached for his pen, pulling it over to her. "Do you mind?"

He shook his head. "Please. Put your thoughts there. We'll amalgamate what we both want to say."

She was quiet for a few moments, re-reading what he had written. Then she looked up, her eyes searching his, seeing the love, trust and compassion as well as the concern and fear he had for her.

"All right. Let's work this through then."

An hour later, Aveleen sat back. "It think this the best we can do. Send it off before either one of us changes our minds."

He leaned to kiss her and then pushed back from the table, the wheels of his chair squealing slightly as he moved. She watched for a moment, her hands rubbing up and down her arms before she looked at her fingers. They had threatened to break each one and promised if she ever talked that would be exactly what they would do. Lord, I can't live in fear. Not any more. Please, dear Lord, let this end?

The next morning, Frankie stood in the kitchen of the cabin, a dark look on his face. "You really went and did this? I didn't think you would. Have you thought through the consequences?"

"We talked about it, Frankie. Why are you so surprised?" Logan shared a look with Aveleen.

"I know we did, but I didn't really expect you to do that." Frankie shook his head, before he waved his hands in the air and then walked away.

"He's definitely not happy, is he?" Aveleen walked to the window and watched as he drove away from the cabin.

Logan stared down at the paper, conflicted as to whether they had done the right thing. Even with the column in print, he wasn't sure.

Aveleen leaned against him, her arm around his shoulders as she read his column.

"The Pioneer by Logan Carmichael

"Today, my column is different. It's not about what I've been up to. But then again it is. You, my readers, know that I suffered a life-changing incident but I have never spoken about it. You know as well that I found the love of my life and settled in Riverville, her hometown. What you don't know is the danger and fear she has been living with since before I met her.

"A few months ago, I scaled down a cliff, finding my bride unconscious at the base. I had no idea who it was. We ended up being abducted again, or I should say, I was. She had never gotten away from her abductors. We were rescued, details of which I cannot and will not put out there as the investigation is still ongoing.

"My bride has lived in fear, constantly, with her family, my family, friends being threatened over and over and over again. We have been followed. Photos have been sent. Warning letters. All of which are in the police hands and under their investigation.

"On our wedding day, my bride was abducted for a second time. During that time she was beaten over and over. It is only by God's grace that she survived. Where she was rescued from and how is not for disclosure here. During this time, I took a bullet, literally, for her brother. That has left me a cripple, in a wheelchair. For the rest of my life? Only God knows that outcome of that.

"We are still living in fear every day. My bride looks over her shoulder every single time she steps out of a building. She should not live in fear like that. I live in fear that I will lose the sweetest thing in my life.

"For those who abducted her, for those who threatened everyone around her, for those who are stalking us, hear me and hear me well. Your time is limited. You will be caught and face the consequences of what you have done. It is only a matter of time. May God have mercy on your souls, because right now, I'm not sure I can."

She looked up. "It says so much, but doesn't give anything away. Will it help? Will it bring them out?"

Logan shrugged, his hand tightening on hers. "I pray this is over and soon. We need to go on with our lives and we can't. Not with this hanging over our heads. Even if we moved across the country or to a totally different country, they would only follow us."

"They would. That's what makes me so angry at times. They control our lives. And I don't like that."

Logan nodded at the vehemence in her words. "They do. But I think this will bring a resolution to them. They're bullies. Bullies will run when confronted in the right way. I just pray this will have been the right way." He looked around the cabin. "This is nice. Abe has done a great job on the renovations."

"He has. He took over the company from his father. They used to go out on security assignments all the time but he and Murphy decided that when the men started to marry and then knowing there would be children involved they would no longer travel like that, putting the men at risk. He's become well known for his excellent training in security. They still go out at times but it is rare. Elizabeth told me she is so glad. Nathaniel's the sniper on the team and he has never had to fire on any one. There is always a chance he will if they continue going in to bring out people."

"That there is." Logan reached and pulled her down into the chair with him, his arms tight around her. "We need to talk about things, Aveleen."

"What things?   I thought we had talked about everything."

"We have, but there is one thing we haven't talked about. Pets."

She froze. "No dogs. I'm sorry. I can't do dogs."

"I get that. How about a cat?" He watched with interest, a smile playing around his mouth, as she thought through that.

"That might work, but it would have to be a special cat." She frowned, turning her head. "Do I hear a cat?"

"I think you might." He shoved at the wheels, stopping in front of the bathroom door and shoving it open. "There's a kitten in there. Now, how did that ever happen?"

"Logan!" She turned to look down, a softened look on her face. "Oh! A little calico. A girl I am assuming. Whose is she?"

"Yours." She hardly heard his word, turning to frown at him, seeing the pleasure on his face that the kitten was bringing her.

"Logan? How? Where'd you get her?"

"Frankie found her for me. She's about nine weeks old. And she's yours. If you want her."

Aveleen reached to pick up the kitten, her face rubbing against the fur. "Oh, I do. I've always wanted a calico kitten but just never took the step." She held the kitten up to stare at her face. "She's adorable."

"And yes, she's yours. You get to name her." He laughed at she shook a finger at him. "Frankie brought her out this morning for me, as well as a bunch of supplies for her."

"Thank you." She leaned to kiss him quickly before turning back to the kitten. "I'll have to think about a name." She began to laugh. "Definitely not Meow One."

Logan began to laugh. "Meow One? What are you talking about?"

"Emma rescued a kitten once and kept telling it she could meow, too, as she would only purr. Abe kept calling her Meow Too." She grinned at the memory of hearing that. "Abe does have a soft heart, underneath."

"I know he does." He sighed as he heard a knock at the door. "Now, who were we expecting today?"

"No one that I know of." She peered around him as she called come in and Murphy entered, pausing as he saw the kitten in her hands.

"No! Please! Not Meow One!"

Aveleen and Logan broke out into laughter. "No, not that."

Chapter 31

Caleb walked towards Logan a week later after church. Logan and Aveleen had moved back to her house, knowing that they needed to decide where they would actually live. Logan watched as Caleb made his way through the crowd, stopping to talk with the people of his town.

He finally reached Logan and sat in a nearby chair. "This is hard work, you know." He laughed at the grin Logan sent his way. "How are you two?"

"So far, we doing okay. No response to the column."

"Yes. That column. Did you really think it would bring them out?" Caleb had been concerned when he read it.

"It will. It just isn't time yet." He reached into his shirt pocket. "Here. This was on the front porch this morning. Aveleen refused to pick it up."

"Another one?" Caleb opened it carefully, his face paling under his tan. "Did you read this?"

Logan shook his head. "No. I didn't open it. But it wasn't sealed." He watched Caleb's attempt to compose himself. "Caleb?"

"Your column is working. This is a direct reference to what you put in there." He rose and began to pace. "Now, what do I do with you two? I can't let you go home without someone to watch over you."

Logan sighed. "We talked about that, Aveleen and I. I guess it's come to that, hasn't it?"

"It has. I'm sending you back to Abe until we can come up with a plan." Caleb looked up to see Aveleen standing behind Logan, her hands on his shoulders. "Aveleen?"

"No, Caleb. I'm not running. Not any more."

He nodded, knowing that was how she would react. "Okay, then. Let me make some calls." He walked away, his phone to his ear.

"Do we have to wait, Logan?"

"I think we need to give him that, Sweetest. He's only thinking of keeping you alive and well." Logan didn't put the rest of his thoughts into words, but his thoughts were that this was it. One or both of them might not survive. Let Aveleen survive, Lord. Take me if someone has to die.

Aveleen paced the living room at home. Caleb had finally let them leave the church, their vehicle in the middle of a convoy of patrol vehicles. She had protested when she finally faced him that he had gone overboard, that the convoy had been too much. He had just given the look he liked to give and walked away, leaving her words of protest following him.

Logan watched as she paced, wishing he could do the same. He sighed. This was not the time to be crippled, he thought. How could he protect his love from a wheelchair? Sure, he could run them down or run over them, but it wasn't the same.

Aveleen finally stopped in the centre of the room, her eyes on Logan, waiting for him to speak.

"Logan? Now what? We're prisoners, aren't we?" She could feel the panic starting to rise once more within her.

"No, we're not prisoners. I've told Caleb you will not be kept housed, that you need to be able to come and go. That if he tried to put you away somewhere, it would be like you had been abducted again. And I wouldn't let him do that to you."

She stared at him. "You understand? You told Caleb? He wouldn't take that well?"

"He did. He hadn't realized that was how you would feel. He's trying to work something out to keep you safe and yet let you have freedom."

"Thank you, my love. You have described exactly how I feel." She turned to pace again. "But until they contact us, what do we do?"

"We live our lives. You have your work. I have mine. We continue with what we would normally do. In fact, I want to take you out on a date for supper tonight." He grinned as she spun, her mouth opening and closing.

"A date? Logan, we're married. Married people don't date."

"We can. Mom and Dad always went out on a date once a week. Dad told me a few years ago that they needed the time just for them. It didn't matter if it was a walk in the park eating an ice cream cone. All that mattered was that he was with Mom and she with him and they could talk about whatever came to their minds, or just stay silent, enjoying the love between them. That's how I see our marriage."

She had come to him, sinking down beside him, her chin resting the hands she had on the arm of the chair. "That is so sweet. I could see the love between them. They have it right. Anyone can have a wedding but it takes work and love to make a marriage."

Two days later, they awoke to a normal day. It was early, Aveleen knew, as she rose and dressed, leaving Logan still sleeping, knowing he would awaken shortly. He always woke up once she had risen. If he needed her, he would call for her, that she knew.

She stopped at the front window, pulling the drapes open, seeing the sun just peeking over the horizon, shining through the almost bare branches. Fall had come, she thought. It would soon be Christmas, their first Christmas together, and she needed to start her planning. She didn't see the man standing across from her house, out in the open, no fear on his face.

A few hours later, Logan pushed himself away from the computer and headed for the kitchen. He needed to do something and decided that baking something was just what he needed to do. His mother had believed that boys as well as girls needed to know how to cook and bake. Some of his fondest memories were of being in the kitchen with her. He finally turned from shoving a pan of brownies into the oven and worked to clean up his mess. He could hear the soft singing from Aveleen as she worked away in the office. She had refused to tell him what she was up to, but he knew it was personal, not work. She seemed more relaxed that day, more than he had seen in a long while, and he liked that. He glanced at the clock. His baking would be done in an hour. That would let them head for the diner in town and lunch out. He had made a commitment to himself that he wanted to treat her to dinners, walks, chocolates, and flowers, whatever it was that a man gave the woman he was courting. She had missed out on that and he didn't want that to be a regret. He aimed to make their marriage a lifelong courtship.

Aveleen turned as the odour of the baked brownies drifted through the house and rose, heading to find them. Logan handed her one, knowing that was what she had come for, and laughed at the look of pure joy on her face as she ate it.

"I think you can make these every day. They are so good." Aveleen went to reach for another one, surprised that he stopped her.

"Not every day. That would grow old. But how about going out on a date with me? Lunch at the diner?"

She finally nodded. "I guess. We can't hide, that much we have decided. How dressy?"

With that comment, he knew what she was asking. "On second thought, let's go fancy. Dress up as much as you want to. I think I can manage a suit for a few hours."

Her look of pleasure reassured him he had made the right decision. He waited for her to finish, giving a whistle when she appeared, her light yellow dress flowing around her calves, her hair pulled back at the sides, a heavy shawl completing her outfit.

"You are so beautiful, Sweetest. What did I do to deserve you?"

She just smiled and dropped a kiss on his cheek. "And you are so handsome, you do know that? Where to?"

"We can still go to the diner, unless you would rather go somewhere else."

"No, Mac's is fine.   Did you know he's related to Abe?"

Logan paused, not having been told that. "I didn't know, but it makes sense."

He watched carefully as she ate, noting that her appetite had improved. He stared down at his own meal, his stomach churning from a sense of danger, but knowing that he had to eat. He sighed to himself, looking up to find kind eyes on him. He asked who it was, Aveleen turning to look.

"Eddie and Peg. And Ben and Marg. Retired officers. They are two that I told you about. Eddie is Abe's uncle. And Ben is related to someone, I just can't think at the moment. Being out with my handsome husband has shaken my mind up." She grinned at he shook a finger at her. "I remember. Eddie's is Abe's uncle. Ben is uncle to Frankie's Deirdre. His son is Timothy, who is married to Rachel. She's sister-in-law to Rebecca."

He knew she was flirting with him and liked that. It showed she had relaxed enough to do just that. He reached for her hand, stilling her motions for a moment.

"Thank you, Sweetest. Thank you for trusting me with your heart and your memories. We'll make many more, that will help wipe out the bad ones."

"I know we will. I'm just impatient to have this behind us."

She finally rose, walking beside him, a hand on his shoulder, not seeing the looks that came their way. She was admired and loved by those who knew her. That love would be tested in the next few hours.

"Where to now? We have to work, you know?"

"We plan hooky for a few hours. We can work this evening. At least you can. I'm all caught up." He grinned at her look. "No? Doesn't work that way?"

"No, it means I'm all caught up to. This is also something we need to talk about. Do I still work from home or find a job in an office? I like this online stuff I'm doing. It's a challenge but I can work what hours I want."

"Then, keep it up for now. We can also readdress this issue later."

Logan looked around as they walked towards the car. Aveleen waited until he had slid into the car, not shutting the door, her hand on the handle of the wheelchair, sensing someone coming towards her. She looked up, a small scream torn from her. She turned, blindly beginning to run, knowing that she didn't have time to get into the car. Her shoes came off and she fled on her stocking feet, feeling the gravel cutting into the tender soles before she hit the grass and continued to run, leading whoever it was away from Logan. She didn't hear his shouts or see him struggling back into his chair, his arms pumping as he desperately tried to catch up with them. She didn't hear the shouts from the male diners who had rushed out to see what was going on or hear the shouts for her to come back, they would help her. She didn't hear the yells for someone to call the police.

Chapter 32

Her heart racing, Aveleen continued to run, stumbling at times as she tried to keep her feet. She didn't notice how close her pursuer had gotten until she was suddenly taken to the ground, his weight holding her there even as she sobbed for him to let her go. He laughed at her distress, stating he was there to finish what he hadn't finished before.

"You're not walking away this time. No one will come find you and rescue you." He forgot that he was in the middle of town, that men were running his way. His fist came back and drove with all his strength into her face.

She cried with pain as she felt her jaw give way and her vision darkened. She didn't see the fist come back again and again. She didn't hear Logan calling for her assailant to stop or hear his taunts back.

Logan's wheelchair stopped abruptly at the grassy edge of the parking lot and he shouted for the man to leave Aveleen alone.

To take him on instead. The man, no youth, Logan thought, turned with an evil grin and taunts.

"Not happening, cripple. You can't stop me. See? She's dead already." He turned from Logan, not seeing Logan lever himself to the front of his chair, his feet hitting the ground.

Logan didn't hesitate, didn't stop to think that he couldn't walk, and launched himself across the grass, his weight hitting the youth, sending the younger man to the ground. He used his own weight to hold the youth down, his hand on the man's right arm, twisting it up behind his back, his other hand on the side of the man's head, grinding it into the grass.

"No. This is enough. You've done enough damage to her. Now, you pay." Logan felt a hand on his shoulder and looked up.

Frankie stood there, shock on his face. "Let me have him, Logan. Aveleen needs you."

Logan gave one final shove at the youth, and then tumbled off him, crawling to where Aveleen lay still. Dave and his partner, Tom, were there, already working to stabilize her. Dave stared at Logan for a moment, watching as Logan reached to touch Aveleen.

"Dave? How is she?"

"He broke her jaw. That much I know. What other damage he did we'll find out at the hospital." Dave shared a look with Frankie before he spoke again. "Logan? How did you get over here? Your chair's back there, what fifteen or twenty feet away? You didn't crawl here."

Logan sat back, his back burning and pain beginning to darken his face. "I have no idea, Dave. But my back hurts." He collapsed back, sending Tom to his side. "Tom?"

"I would say you're able to walk again. But I don't know what damage you've done. Lie still." Tom's hand shoved him back down. "I said, lie still. You're not doing anyone any good moving around. You may well damage what has been healed."

Five hours later, Logan sat beside Aveleen's hospital bed, her hand in his, not taking his eyes from her. She had been taken to surgery to repair her jaw. The surgeon had given Frankie a black look when he described her injury, asking did Frankie know her jaw was broken in two places and he really didn't know if they could save her teeth? Frankie had shuddered before he turned to ask about Logan.

The physician had shaken his head, simply stating that he had no answers for what had happened, other than Logan's healing had been complete and he had just needed a push to walk again. But he wouldn't have recommended that very type of push.

Logan looked up as Frankie stopped by the bed, his gaze resting on Aveleen before he spoke.

"How is she?"

"She hasn't been awake but they don't expect that for a while, not until the anesthesia wears off. I don't know how I got over there, Frankie. I really don't."

"I talked to Mac. He was heading your way when you just stood up and ran towards Aveleen. He said he has never seen anything like that." Frankie looked around. "How's the back?"

"It hurts, but the physician said I didn't do any damage to it. Thank God for that. I just wish it hadn't taken this to get me on my feet again."

"If you had been on your feet, this wouldn't have ended today." Frankie paused, searching for words. "We have all the men now. The oldest was the one today. He's only twenty. The rest are eighteen or younger."

"Kids. Just kids. Why? They should be out having fun, not destroying lives."

"That's what we have to fully determine, but one of the younger ones said drugs were offered to them, drugs, alcohol, money. They thought it was a game. They had no concept that real life is different from their video games. That if they hurt people, people could die or at the very least have their lives changed dramatically. There's a connection with the leader to the one behind him, but we haven't quite got there. We have to go to court to have adoption records opened for us."

Aveleen groaned as she turned her head, hearing the conversation, and unable to understand why she couldn't speak.

Logan bent close to her. "What is it, Sweetest? You know the connection?"

She grimaced with pain as she tried her best to make him understand. He raised back up, a dark look on his face before he turned to Frankie, telling him what Aveleen had said.

Frankie stared first at Logan and then at Aveleen, seeing her nod before her eyes slid closed. "I'm off to check this out. There's an officer on the door. Don't leave here. They'll bring in a cot for you, Logan. I need you to stay together. This has just broken loose and she'll come hunting for you two."

Logan watched as the door swished closed behind Frankie before he turned back to Aveleen. The pain in his back was tolerable, he decided, and then slid the bedrail down, crawling up beside her and wrapping her in his arms. He really didn't care if they came and told him he couldn't do that. He was just going to and they could live with it.

Caleb stared at the younger couple two days later. Logan was still using his wheel chair at times, finding he tired easily. Aveleen sat beside him on the couch, a mutinous look on her face.

"You can't do that, Aveleen. You can't be there when we make the arrest."

"I don't care. I need to see her face, for her to know she lost. She may have others out there to come after us and I need to know there aren't any. If she doesn't see me, then she'll think I'm still living in fear. I can't live like that any more, Caleb."

"Logan, talk some sense into her." Caleb appealed to the young husband, knowing it wasn't likely to work.

"Not happening, Caleb. In fact, I want to be there too. I want to look that woman in the eye."

Caleb finally agreed, but only if they stayed back and didn't say a word. He watched as Logan moved his chair through the court house, Aveleen's hand on his shoulder, before it tightened as they stopped in front of a door. Frankie stood there, two officers with him, one a female detective. Caleb nodded to Frankie, who, paperwork in hand, opened the door and walked in, leaving the door open. Caleb moved to a position beside Aveleen, just to be prepared for whatever came next. He knew officers were stationed around them, all volunteering. He had had more than he needed volunteer, the whole force wanting to see this over for Aveleen and Logan.

The lawyer's assistant looked up, a surprised look on her face, as Frankie approached her.

"What can I do for you? Do you have an appointment with Mr. Brown?" Her voice was stern and coarse.

"Lorraine Walker. You're under arrest." Frankie reached for his handcuffs, finding the woman backing away. He sighed. "Don't make it worse for yourself than it already is. You're under arrest for conspiracy to murder, kidnapping, assault, dealing in drugs, providing drugs and alcohol to minors. Where would you like me to stop?"

"I've done none of that." She looked up as the lawyer stepped out of his office, a question on his face. "Mr. Brown. I have done nothing wrong."

"What are the charges again, Officer?"

Frankie repeated them, hearing a slight movement behind him. He watched as the woman's face paled and then fell, and he knew that Aveleen had moved up behind him, the very sight of her letting Lorraine Walker know she had been found out. There was no way out for her now.

Aveleen watched as the older woman was handcuffed and led away, her arm around Logan as he stood beside her, his arms wrapping her in a feeling of security. Caleb finally touched her arm and she nodded. It was over, she prayed. Over except to testify in court. That she could do. Now she could start to live her life. Her steps stumbled as tears blinded her eyes. Caleb's hand under her arm held her upright as did her grip on Logan's shoulder.

Logan watched later as she slept, traces of tears on her cheeks. He lay beside her, his arms once more holding her close, his heart broken for his bride, but thankful that she was finally free of the hurt, the fear, the terror, the threats. His heart raised in prayer and praise for her and he too slept,

his cheek against her hair.   They needed
time, he knew, time to heal.

Chapter 33

Turning from her gardens in the early spring, Aveleen rose, stretching, enjoying the warmth of the sun. She felt revived, knowing that Lorraine Walker was now incarcerated and would not be out for many years. It had been revealed at her trial that the older youth was her son, one she had given up for adoption as a teen mother. She had resented the fact that he had taken her from the life she had planned as a teenager and used him to seek revenge on anyone she felt had been against her.

How she focused her venom on Aveleen was still a puzzle to some. She had been jealous of the younger woman, who was well loved in her home town, her character matching her beauty. She had felt slighted by many and had fixated on Aveleen. Why she had chosen her, that had come out in the trial, even though there were some who doubted the veracity of it.

Aveleen had given her testimony in the courts, the details of what she had suffered at the hands of the youths not known to many and no one person, other than the police officials and Logan, knowing the full extent of the abuse and terror she had been subjected to. She had stared at Lorraine Walker as she spoke.

The woman had sputtered and cursed, her true character finally revealed. It became known that she had been a supplier of drugs to the young people in town, who would do just about anything she asked to have a ready supply. These youths had been behind the swarmings, the break-ins, the thefts, the terror that had the police baffled for months. It had come out that she had hired the original kidnappers, the man in charge of them a friend from her teens. It was rumoured he was the father of her son, but nothing was ever proven. It had also come out that she had taken issue with Logan's columns, not liking what he was writing and somehow putting Aveleen and Logan together in her mind as her enemies, both of whom had to be taken care of.

Aveleen had realized that she knew the men from her work, that they had been in and out of her employer's office on many occasions, as had Lorraine Walker. Aveleen had never spoken directly with them, finding them leaving as she would arrive in the morning, which surprised her.

Aveleen had finally admitted to Logan that she was leaving her employment and likely moving town because she no longer felt comfortable in the office, that something had felt off for a while. The office suite had been searched and cameras and microphones found in her office, planted by the original kidnappers. She couldn't explain to Logan how she and Avery had almost come to a parting of their ways, other than that she felt he was too protective and she felt stifled by him.

Logan had sat and watched his bride as she spoke, his heart heavy for her but praying constantly for her. She had sat back beside him when she finished, her face white, feeling draining, but feeling the peace she always felt from her pioneer. She had laughed one day, calling him that, and asking him how he felt about the journey he had been on. It was not unlike the days of yesteryear when the pioneers crossing the country had faced danger, she stated. He had looked at her and replied that it had been a journey he would gladly have avoided, except he found her on it.

She reached for her calico cat, now almost full grown. She had settled on the name of Keevi, just why she couldn't say. She had no idea where that name had come from but simply stated it suited her crazy calico. She looked up, spying Logan standing, leaning again a post on the back deck, hands in his pockets, a smile on his face just for her. She praised God every day that He had healed him, that he was able to do what he wanted. He refused to let her get rid of the wheelchair, stating he needed it for now.

"Aveleen? Sweetest? Are you done playing in the dirt?" He grinned as she walked up the steps and into his embrace, Keevi protesting before she jumped from Aveleen's arms.

"I am. Why? Do you want a turn?" She grinned at him in return.

"No. It's just Greg called. He asked if we could meet him at the church. He didn't say why."

She looked down at her clothes and the dirt. "Let me change. Fifteen and then we're good to go."

Aveleen's hand was tight in Logan's as they walked into the church, a frown on her face as she found their families there, Abe's men and their ladies, her other friends and their spouses, Doc Aaron, Martha, and Ted. She had no idea what was going on and she didn't think Logan did either.

"Aveleen. Logan." Greg approached them, Mary at his side. "We've wanted to do something for you, to help you make some new memories of your wedding day. We would like to redo your ceremony. The church ladies are busy in the kitchen, preparing a meal for us." He watched as her mouth opened and closed in shock before he spoke again. "That is, if it's what you want. We just thought you needed something. If we've stepped over the line, please forgive us." He waited for them to speak, before he stepped back, a sadness showing briefly on his face.

Logan had been watching Aveleen, and finally spoke, his eyes not leaving her face. "Thank you, Greg. That is exactly what we need. I think you've left Aveleen speechless, for once." He smiled as she frowned at his choice of words. "What have we to do?"

"Well, there are ladies here who raided your closet. Aveleen, if you would like to go with Mary, Kataleen, and Adriel, I believe they have your wedding dress and whatnot in one of the Sunday school rooms. Logan, your brother has your suit in another room."

He looked around for a moment. "There are flowers here. The florist sent them, at no charge. In fact, I think you'll find the church will be full by the time you are ready. If you had said no, we would have just enjoyed a meal together."

Aveleen leaned against Logan later that afternoon, his arms around her. "Did you know?"

He shook his head. "No, I had no idea. This is really sweet of them, you know."

"It is. This is how our church works." She turned her head to look up at him. "I love you, my husband."

"And I you." He kissed her, promises in his very touch. "I want to grow old with you. For a while, I didn't think we'd get a chance to do that."

"God knows why we went through what we did. It was hard. It changed us. It almost destroyed us. But He was gracious and led us to victory. Logan, what now?"

"What now? I have no idea. I'm just along for the ride." He grinned and ducked the elbow she shoved into his ribs. "As to the immediate future, I would say we find that cabin we were to go to, shut out the world and forget that we had an adventure."

"I like that idea but there's a problem. We can't."

He paled, having been sure that she would agree. "We can't? Why not?"

"There's the kitten. We can't leave her home on her own. Who knows what damage she'll do."

Logan began to laugh as his arms tightened around her, causing eyes to find them and smiles to light up faces. "I'm sure someone will look after her. Avery owes me. He can do it."

Avery had approached Logan one day, apologizing once more for his attitude towards him. Logan had looked at him and then hugged him, telling him he understood.

He had a sister who had an attitude like his. Avery had stared at him before he began to laugh, but tears lurked beneath the surface as he thanked Logan again for saving his life, even though it had been devastating for him at the time. Logan had simply shaken his head, replied that God had been in control, and that God knew Logan was better able to handle what had happened. Avery had stared into the distance for a moment before he agreed.

Logan finally reached for Aveleen's hand and walked among the crowd gathered, stopping for hugs and kisses from the ladies, handshakes from most of the men but a few hugs from them as well. Aveleen was content. The man she loved was accepted by her friends and by her town. God has been good, she thought. Now, Lord, just because I said that, I don't want another adventure. And please, Dear Lord, keep our family and friends safe. No more adventures for them either.

Dear Readers:

Thank you for choosing to read The Pioneer, the second book in the Children of His Promise series. It was quite a ride this couple took me on. They just took over the story and told me what to write and who would be appearing in the story.

And it was quite the story to write. Nothing was planned the way it happened. I didn't intend for Aveleen to be abducted a second time, certainly not from her wedding. Logan's injury in saving Avery's life was not planned either, but worked so well into the story and its eventual resolution.

Logan declared himself a modern-day pioneer, seeking new ground to till and new friends to find. He did that so well. He also found that he had to learn and relearn who God is and how He protects us. That is a lesson we all need to learn.

I had no intentions of Caleb's Hannah being a cousin. That Holly and Aveleen told me was to happen. I also had no intention of Abe's team making an appearance or for

Dave to step in as he did.   But it was a pleasure to revisit old characters.

We face danger in many ways, not just physical.   I see youth today who have no concept of life and death.   Abuse, beatings, drugs, alcohol, whatever they are involved with - that is their life today and they have little fear of the consequences. To take a life is not real to them. That saddens me. There are many youths out there that are a pleasure to know but there are also some you don't want to be around. That fact is scary.

While writing this book, I was told that my oldest Sheltie has a non-curable syndrome and that is hard to take.   I will treasure the time I have with her.   That has affected the time I had to take away from writing.

As to the calico kitten, I added a little calico girl in May.   She is a crazy little girl, but such a sweetheart.   Her name is Irish as she was born on March 17, St. Patricks' Day. She is called Caoimhe (Keeva) and her nickname is Keevi.   Of course that had to work its way into the book.   My three Shelties and the two cats and now the kitten

(I lost my older cat in April) all find a way to finagle themselves into a story.

No matter what you face, remember that God loves you, has you written on the palms of His hands and is just a prayer away.

God bless each one of you.

Ronna